"Your bed or mine?" Emily asked

Her eyes were big and glistening with passion.

"Both," Jonah promised her.

And just like that the game ended. Slowly she slipped her nightie off her shoulders, leaving her exposed in all her beauty.

Leaning forward, he decided it was well time he joined in this seduction. He explored her mouth, teasing her lips, making her sigh. He let his mouth go all the places it wanted to go—the swell of her breasts, her nipples, which tasted like heaven.

When he nuzzled her belly, she giggled. "You should have shaved."

"Next time I will...."

She sighed and Jonah felt the quiver of her skin beneath his lips. "I can't believe you didn't jump me the second we got into the room."

"You have no idea how much I wanted to," he murmured into her belly button. "How much I still do..."

Blaze

Dear Reader,

Some things you just can't make up! This book came about after an extremely memorable writing retreat in the Pacific Northwest. My friends and I booked in to a charming lodge to write. One of our rooms had bedbugs and we all had to move. They took away all our clothes and cases to be treated and, since the lodge was full, we got rooms they normally don't rent out. The room that Emily ends up with is pretty much the room I had. Since I couldn't sleep, I played the writer's favorite game. *What if?*

I'm grateful to all my zany writing friends, especially the Duetters, who can always be counted on for laughter and support. A special thanks to Candy Halliday, who helped with the orthodontist background, and to Holly and A.J., who helped in many ways.

As far as I know, there is no Elk Crossing Lodge in Idaho, and if there is I have never been there. The location was entirely fictitious.

Hope you enjoy *Power Play,* my unique contribution to the FORBIDDEN FANTASIES promotion. As always, come visit me on the Web at www.nancywarren.net.

Happy reading,

Nancy Warren

USA TODAY Bestselling Author

Nancy Warren

POWER PLAY

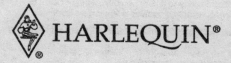

HARLEQUIN®

TORONTO • NEW YORK • LONDON
AMSTERDAM • PARIS • SYDNEY • HAMBURG
STOCKHOLM • ATHENS • TOKYO • MILAN • MADRID
PRAGUE • WARSAW • BUDAPEST • AUCKLAND

Recycling programs
for this product may
not exist in your area.

ISBN-13: 978-0-373-79506-2

POWER PLAY

Copyright © 2009 by Nancy Warren.

www.eHarlequin.com

Printed in U.S.A.

USA TODAY Bestselling Author

Nancy Warren

POWER PLAY

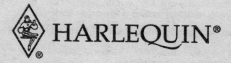

TORONTO • NEW YORK • LONDON
AMSTERDAM • PARIS • SYDNEY • HAMBURG
STOCKHOLM • ATHENS • TOKYO • MILAN • MADRID
PRAGUE • WARSAW • BUDAPEST • AUCKLAND

Recycling programs
for this product may
not exist in your area.

ISBN-13: 978-0-373-79506-2

POWER PLAY

www.eHarlequin.com

Printed in U.S.A.

1

THE SCREAMS WOKE EMILY Saunders. Horror movie worthy shrieks of terror that had her jerking up in bed and panicking for a moment when she didn't immediately recognize her surroundings.

She flicked on the bedside lamp, noting fuzzily that it was 5:07 a.m. The bed and the rest of the hotel room furniture came into focus along with her thoughts. Right. She was back in Elk Crossing, Idaho, in her room at the Elk Crossing Lodge.

For a second she wondered if the screams had been part of a nightmare. Her gaze drifted to the pumpkin-colored bridesmaid dress hanging in the unfortunately see-through bag. No wonder she was having nightmares. When her cousin Leanne had asked her to be a bridesmaid, Emily had said, "Yes, of course." She always said yes.

But she really thought she might have plucked up the courage to turn down the honor of being a bridesmaid had she known about the dresses. Pumpkin—the color—was bad enough, but did the shape of the dress have to resemble the vegetable? Emily had worn some hideous bridesmaid gowns in her time, but this one really took the trick-or-treat candy.

She was about to flick off the light and try to get

back to sleep when she heard more screaming. And it seemed to be coming from right outside her door.

Shoving her feet into her blue terry-towel slippers and grabbing the matching robe off the end of the bed, she picked up her room key and ran to the door. Touch it first, she reminded herself, wishing she'd bothered, for once, to read that "in case of fire" map taped to the back of the door. She didn't feel heat, or smell smoke, but the commotion continued out there in the hallway.

Amid the screams she heard some soothing tones, and nobody seemed to be rushing for exits. Also, no fire alarm rang.

Curiosity had her cautiously opening her door.

The sight that met her eyes was—unusual.

A plump young woman, well-endowed and naturally not wearing a bra in the middle of the night, was jumping up and down as though the carpet of the hotel was a trampoline. She was the one doing the screaming.

"I saw them. Crawling everywhere. They're on me. Eww. Eww," she bellowed.

A much skinnier woman with long arms and legs, wearing a pink baby doll and nothing else, shrieked, "I felt something. I think they're in my hair."

And the pair of them were off, screaming, shaking their heads and bouncing like crazed groupies at a Jonas Brothers concert.

Emily stepped forward, wondering if they were on drugs of some kind.

A young guy in a hotel uniform was trying, with absolutely no success, to calm the women down. "Please, ladies, you're waking the other guests." He looked too young to wear a uniform and a sheen of sweat covered his upper lip.

An older, gray-haired couple who'd put overcoats and outdoor shoes on, stared, as stunned as she. They spoke to each other in soft voices. The woman caught Emily's eye and shrugged in a "what do you do?" kind of way.

While Emily tried to recall what she knew of drug and alcohol poisoning, another door opened across the hall and a big, muscular, hairier-than-necessary man stepped out wearing nothing but boxer shorts with some brand of beer stamped on them. He was in his early thirties, she'd guess, with dark hair that stuck up on one side where he'd slept on it. His gaze took in the scene at once then snagged momentarily on the bouncing breasts.

"They're crawling on me, they're crawling on me," the girl screamed again.

Emily snapped to the useless guy in uniform, "Call 9-1-1. These women need medical attention."

Hairy Guy walked up to the girls, showing everyone in the hallway an excellent physique. Muscular, hard and drool-worthy, his near naked bod oozed testosterone and reminded her that she hadn't had sex in far too long. "You don't need 9-1-1," he said in a low, bottom-of-the-gravel-pit voice. "You need an exterminator."

Before her bemused gaze, he reached forward and plucked something from the plump girl's shoulder. He held a flat black speck out on the edge of his finger. It was the size of a flax seed. He showed it to the flustered fellow in uniform.

"Bedbugs."

By this time, more doors had opened along the corridor. A traveling salesman type yawned. "What's going on?"

The couple in overcoats announced in unison, in horrified accents, "Bedbugs."

The uniformed guy swallowed. Then looked up at the man in boxer shorts with appeal. "But the hotel's full."

"Not for long."

Emily took a step away from the girls who were standing in shocked stillness. She didn't blame them for looking so horrified.

Bedbugs? This was all she needed, on top of driving all the way from Portland to Elk Crossing for a wedding she didn't want to attend with far too many of her family and friends asking nosy questions about her own continuing single status. This was the icing on the already hideous wedding cake. Decorated, she now recalled, with walnut-size marzipan pumpkins. And a tiny bride and groom perched on top, surrounded by faux fall leaves. No doubt by the actual wedding day, somebody would have thought to add a horn of plenty.

The thin girl lifted her arm. "I'm so itchy." Even from across the hall Emily could see small red welts. And they were swelling.

Her irritation at the entire situation instantly changed to sympathy. "Let me see if I can find you some antihistamines," she said.

Hairy Guy glanced her way and nodded in approval. Then he spoke to the two women, now both compulsively scratching.

"Go in the bathroom, strip off and shower in hot water. Hot as you can stand. Don't put any of your clothes back on."

He glanced at the hotel employee. "Get a female to bring them fresh towels and some clean robes."

The guy nodded and trotted off. Fast.

With a hiccup and a "This is soo disgusting" the two women went back into their room.

"You," he called to the useless guy in uniform who was already halfway down the hall. "You'd better get hold of the hotel manager."

"This is not good," Emily muttered, as she dug out her traveling medical kit. She'd had a tough enough time getting her family to accept that she wouldn't be bunking down in some distant relative's overflowing basement for the duration of the wedding festivities. Years of experience had taught her that she could manage her massive family if she stayed in a hotel. Wasn't it exactly her luck to pick one with an insect problem?

She took the antihistamines over to the bedbug-infested room and knocked on the door. When the slimmer of the two women answered, wrapped in a towel, she held out the package. "Here." She dropped the box into the girl's outstretched hand.

"Thanks. I'll take a few out and—"

"No, no. Keep them. They're yours. Hope you feel better soon," she said, and speedily retraced her steps back to her room.

Fifteen minutes had passed since she'd been woken. For a nanosecond she contemplated getting back into bed, then recalled the sight of that tiny insect on the guy's finger.

She dashed to her bed and yanked down the covers, searching. Her sheets looked perfectly white. Nothing moving.

Her hair brushed her cheek and the slight tickle had her jumping and scratching at her face. No way she was getting back into that bed. Her sleep for the night was clearly over.

Her next stop was the bathroom where she stripped off and looked at herself from every angle. No bugs that she could see. No bites. She breathed a sigh of relief and stepped into the shower, running it long and hot and washing her hair and body twice over.

Her mom must never find out about the vermin, she resolved as water ran over her body. Unfortunately, her mom and dad were already in Elk Crossing mostly so her mom could support her sister, Emily's aunt Irene, in marrying off her daughter. As close as the two women were, Em knew it was killing her mother to see Irene's daughter, Leanne, get married first. Since Leanne was more than five years younger than her own very unmarried—as in didn't even have a steady boyfriend—daughter.

Naturally, they were staying at wedding central. A place Emily had already decided she'd spend as little time in as possible for the next week. Not that she didn't love her family, but all that wistful longing and those unsubtle hints were hard on a girl.

She inspected the towel on the rail and then shook it vigorously before toweling herself dry.

There was a knock on her door. Wrapping the damp towel around her, she opened the door to a sleepy-looking chambermaid. "We're very sorry, ma'am, but you'll need to vacate your room." The girl—she doubted she was even out of her teens—held a large, green Rubbermaid bin in her hands.

"No problem." As if she'd sleep there another minute. "Just let me get dressed and get my stuff."

"Um. You can't."

"I beg your pardon?"

The girl stepped inside and shut the door. Then she peeled the lid off the bin. Only now did Emily see that across the lid in faded black Sharpie ink were the words: *Lost and Found. Women's.*

"You have got to be kidding me."

"I'm real sorry. But we have to launder everything, and treat your cases, too." She stuck a fake bright smile on her face. "I'm sure there's something in the lost and found bin that will fit you."

"But, I don't have bedbugs. I'm sure my room is fine."

"I'm only doing what the manager told me to, ma'am. We're evacuating and treating this entire wing. You want I should call him?"

"No. No." She understood that they had to contain the infestation, and fast. The last thing she wanted was to be the unwitting bearer of bedbugs to her cousin's wedding.

She looked inside.

The clothes inside that plastic tub were the kind that if you forgot them at a hotel you wouldn't care enough to go back and retrieve them. Faded track pants, ancient sweatshirts, a bright pink faux silk blouse from the seventies, old jeans, some workout wear, a floral housecoat. A handful of bathing suits.

Emily couldn't help herself. She started to laugh. She saw herself showing up to today's prewedding event, which was lunch and then some kind of craft project that involved making paper roses for the wedding. No doubt orange ones. When she imagined herself showing up in crumpled lost and found clothing, when her mother was always boasting about how successful she was, she laughed until she snorted.

The chambermaid stared at her as though she'd lost her mind, which only made her laugh harder. Finally, she wiped her eyes and thought: emergency shopping trip. "I'm going to need my purse."

"Just your wallet. Leave everything else in the room. I'm really sorry, but we have to contain this."

Stuff happened, Emily reminded herself. Then had a terrible thought.

"My bridesmaid gown. It's in a plastic bag, it'll be okay, won't it?"

The girl looked doubtfully at the dress, clearly visible in its see-through bag and then back at Emily, as though wondering why anyone would want to save that gown. If it weren't for the family thing, Em would agree with her.

"I know. It's butt ugly, but if I don't wear that dress down the aisle on Saturday for my cousin's wedding, I might as well cross my name out of the family bible. You know what I mean?"

Fervent nodding. "I'll ask the manager. He'll know what to do."

"Is the Elk Mall still the only shopping center in town? Oh, and I'll need a list of other hotels."

She'd last been in town a few months ago for a twenty-fifth wedding anniversary. Her mom had moved away from Elk Crossing before Emily was even born, but she'd dragged the family back so many times over the years that Emily knew the town pretty well.

While she was speaking, the young girl dug down into the bin and handed her a pair of black polyester satin pants, the pink polyester silk shirt and a fluorescent-green windbreaker with a tear in the pocket.

Emily looked at the crumpled garments hanging from her hand. "Can I at least wear my underwear?"

"No. Everything gets washed." The girl sent her another sunny smile. "But these are all clean. We always wash them before they go in the lost and found."

"That's good to know." Especially since she'd be going commando.

"Yep, Elk Mall's still the place. It has a Wal-Mart now," she added with pride. "And we're finding you another room. We should have you settled in a couple hours. Your clothes need to be separated into washable and dry-clean-only piles."

"I don't want another room in this hotel," Emily said in the pleasant but firm tone she used on her massage therapy clients who didn't do their exercises. "I want a list of other local hotels."

"Won't do you any good. They're all full."

"Every hotel room in Elk Crossing is full?" This town was so insignificant it only appeared on regional maps, but she didn't think it was that small. The wedding was adding a hundred people, tops, and most of them were billeted. "I don't mind driving."

The chambermaid shook her head. "Not a hotel room, motel room or bed-and-breakfast is left. Even the campgrounds are full. There's nothing for fifty miles. It's the Over-Thirties Hockey Tourney this week. They've booked everything."

Emily pushed a wet curl back off her forehead. "Tell me you have some good news."

"Sure. Your room's comped. And we're serving free coffee and breakfast in the restaurant."

She sighed. As good news went, she hadn't exactly won the lottery. "What time does Wal-Mart open?"

2

ONLY THE THOUGHT OF BEDBUGS got Emily out of her room once she'd forced herself to dress in the lost and found clothes. The polyester silk pants were too short, ending about three inches from her ankles, but making up in width what they lacked in length, so she'd had to use a safety pin to hold the waistband in place.

By contrast, the shirt was too small, and she was braless. Which was the only reason she finally slipped her arms into the bright green windbreaker.

Unable to resist, she looked at herself in the full-length mirror and tried to see the humor in the situation, but at the moment, she didn't feel like laughing. She looked like a scarecrow that had been left out one winter too many. Loads of her family lived here in Elk Crossing and she had friends here. She had her pride, and her mother's pride in her to think of. They simply could not see her like this.

The only plan she had was to hit Wal-Mart the second it opened, grab something and scoot into the change room. If she could do that, her vanity would be partly spared.

She opened her door and slipped into the hallway, casting one last look at her clothes, neatly separated into wash and dry-clean piles. Naturally, she'd brought her best clothes with her for the interminable wedding breakfasts, lunches, rehearsal dinners, stagette night and whatever other events her inventive relatives could come up with. When someone in her family got married, they liked to drag the thing out at least a week.

She made her way to the restaurant and found about a dozen refugees from her part of the hotel standing around drinking coffee, looking like a convention of hobos. As she entered, the hairy guy who'd diagnosed the bedbug problem glanced up and took in her outfit with interest. Something about his regard made her conscious of her underwearless state, which made her snappish.

Especially as he'd somehow snagged an oversize navy sweater and jeans. Apart from the fact that his jeans didn't go much closer to his ankles than her satin pants, he could pass for normally dressed. She poured herself coffee from an urn and turned to him. "How did you score clothes that actually fit?"

He snorted and lifted the huge sweater. Apart from noticing the same gorgeous abs she'd sighted earlier, she saw a widely gaping fly and, since he was also going commando, she got the impression that his chest wasn't the only place he was impressively hairy.

"I do up this zipper, I'll be singing soprano for the rest of my life," he informed her, and then dropped the sweater back in place. "Did you get bitten?"

"No. You?"

He shook his head. "Far as I can tell, it's only the two women with bites."

"Are they going to be okay?"

He nodded. "They took both of them to the clinic to be looked at, one of them had some kind of reaction, but they should be fine."

She shuddered.

A waitress came out of the kitchen bearing a tray of Danish and fruit.

As she helped herself to a Danish, Emily asked the waitress, "What time does the Wal-Mart open?"

"Seven."

"It's going to be a long hour," she muttered.

The traveling salesman type, wearing faded blue track pants that said *Dancer* across the butt, a red soccer jersey with a bleach stain on the chest and his bare feet stuck into sneakers, suddenly bellowed, while indicating his new outfit, "Would you buy insurance from this man?"

His comment broke the ice and as they all laughed, the bedbug refugees began trading stories and lamenting the bad clothing, bonding over the disaster.

By five to seven, Emily was in the shopping center parking lot, as close as she could get to the Wal-Mart entrance. The minute the doors were unlocked, she put her head down and ran for the entrance. Once inside, she headed straight for the women's clothing section.

She found a simple black skirt and flipped through a rack of silky tank tops, almost weeping when she thought of the suitcase of her good clothes that was currently at the local dry cleaner's mercy.

Naturally, the underwear was in a different area of the store, but she found the intimate apparel at last and was flipping through the bras when a voice said, "Can I help you with anything?"

"No, thanks," she said, not raising her head, hoping desperately the woman with the vaguely familiar voice would move on.

She felt the warm air stirring around her, almost as

though the woman's breath was surrounding her as she stood rooted to the spot.

"Emily Saunders, is that you?"

Oh, crap. Her worst nightmare had just been realized. She raised her head and thought that in a list of the top ten people she would have wanted to avoid at this moment, Ramona Hilcock would have made the top three.

"Ramona!" she cried with false delight.

"I almost didn't recognize you," the woman said, looking her up and down with barely disguised revulsion.

Ramona had been a friend of her younger cousin Leanne's in high school. Emily remembered her as a gossip and president of the sewing club. She still sewed, and Emily was willing to bet, from the way the woman eyed her outfit as though storing every detail, still gossiped.

"You here for Leanne's wedding?"

"Mmm-hmm."

"Oh, good. I'm getting off shift early today, to attend the lunch. Of course, I only work here part-time so I can pay for the boys' music and golf lessons. And it gets me out of the house." Her gaze strayed to Emily's outfit once more. "How about you? I think your mom said you have your own business? Things going okay?"

"Yes. Fine."

She could tell Ramona about the bedbugs, which would explain the lost and found bin wardrobe, but then news would spread faster than an Internet rumor and she'd be staying on some distant relative's couch by tonight. So she kept her mouth shut.

"You're a masseuse, Leanne said." Ramona uttered

the word *masseuse* in a tone that suggested it was synonymous with *rub and tug*.

"Massage therapist," Emily corrected. "I run a wellness clinic." Before Ramona could say another word, she said, "Is there a place I can try these on?"

"Sure. Follow me."

Thankfully, she retreated into the change room where she found everything fit. She paid and was released from Ramona's clutches—until lunch.

Her clothes might not be up to her usual fashion standard, but they were bright and clean and, apart from the Wal-Mart, the local mall had an accessories store and a midrange shoe store. Necessity might be the mother of invention, but it wasn't the mother of fashion. Still, she'd done her best, dressing up the black skirt with a bright scarf belt and hoping some cheap and cheerful costume jewelry would add enough pizzazz to the turquoise tank top.

And it was always nice to stock up on new bras and underwear at a good price, she reminded herself as she headed off to eat lunch and construct paper roses.

JONAH BETTS SLAMMED THE PUCK into the net, watching that baby fly home as if it had a homing device. The punch of puck against black net, the lighting up of the goal light were right up there with sex for truly sublime experiences.

He threw his gloved hand in the air, and his buddies skated over to congratulate him, their blades sawing the ice.

The Old-Timers Hockey League playoff week was one of the highlights of his year. He'd always had more than his share of energy and nothing challenged him more than hockey. He liked the scrape of steel blades on ice, the speed, the male camaraderie, the teamwork.

When the guys bashed him on the helmet, threw themselves at him, he laughed. So it was an exhibition game. Who cared? Tomorrow they'd be playing for real. And, as team captain of the defending champions, he planned to kick some ass.

After a pizza dinner and a couple of beers to celebrate the victory of the Portland Paters over the Georgetown Geezers he hauled his gym bag to his truck, tossed it into the back and headed back to his hotel. Bedbug Lodge. He didn't think he'd been bitten and wondered idly how the two women who'd woken him so spectacularly at five this morning were doing now.

Since his gym bag had been in the truck, he hadn't had to give it up to the fumigators. But he couldn't leave it there tonight, not since he'd used the contents. He needed to take out his skate liners and let them dry, keep his equipment warm. He'd made a quick stop on the way to the rink to pick up some sweats, a new pair of jeans, a couple of T-shirts and socks and underwear, so he was all set. Good as new. He hoisted his bag over his shoulder, grabbed his stick and hiked inside.

"How's it going?" he said to one of the two harried front desk clerks.

He got a pathetically grateful smile. "It's been a busy day. Thank you for your patience, sir." The reply suggested to him that everybody hadn't been as easy to deal with.

"So long as you've got a bed for me, I'm easy. Jonah Betts."

"Even our computers have been overloaded today.

But I managed to get you a room." She glanced up. "Number 318. It's the last one, I'm afraid. We don't normally rent it out, and I've been instructed to comp the room." She sighed, and he suspected she'd done a lot of that in the past twelve hours or so. "We are very sorry."

"Not your fault." He took his key, picked up his bag. Then turned back. "Why don't you rent it out?"

"There's a small leak in the ceiling, sir. But otherwise the room is very comfortable. Two beds, ensuite."

"So long as there's one bed and a TV, I'm good."

She laughed, in relief, he thought. "Oh, yes. TV. Movies. Everything."

He nodded acceptance. "Have a good one."

He hoped there was a fridge in room 318 to keep his beer cold. He should have asked. He followed the clerk's directions to the third floor and strolled along the corridor to the last door.

He opened it with his key card and walked inside.

A woman screamed.

His day had started this way. He really didn't need the bookend.

He dropped his bag with a thunk and regarded the woman who was doing the screaming. Well, more like a cry of alarm. She'd stopped pretty fast and was glaring at him instead.

It was the woman from this morning. The cute one from across the hall. She wore pajamas so new they still had the creases from the package. Blue and manly looking, which only accentuated her woman's body.

He noticed a mane of sleek brown, big dark eyes and a mouth made to whisper dirty secrets.

"Hi," he said. "What are you doing here?"

"I think you've got the wrong room."

He looked down at his key card. Of course, it had no number, but the little folder did. "Weird that the key worked. I'm in room 318." He checked the number on the door. Yep, 318.

She shook her head. "Not possible. *I'm* in 318."

He glanced around the room. It was nice enough. *Cozy,* he supposed was the word, with two queen-size beds and not a lot of space for anything else. There was a small desk with a lamp, a dormer window looking over the woods behind the lodge, a partially open door into a bathroom and, incongruously, where the fourth wall ought to have been, a curtain made of white tarpaulin.

He walked across the room and pulled back the curtain far enough to see the buckets. There were half a dozen twenty-gallon plastic tubs, the kind that store pickles and condiments for industrial kitchens. The wooden beams above showed extensive water damage. Not quite the small leak he'd been told to expect.

"The girl who checked me in said they don't normally rent this room because of the leaky roof," he said, thinking that a new roof for this old lodge was going to cost a fortune.

"That's what the young man who checked me in said." She turned back to what she'd been doing when he'd come in, cutting the tags off an assortment of new clothes. "You'd better go back to the front desk and get another room."

But his mama hadn't raised any fools. If you didn't count his older brother Steven. "They told me this was the last room."

"Well, I was here first."

"I'll call down and get them to send someone up."

She glared at him. She could patent that glare, it was so good. "What is the point? This room is taken."

He'd never been in the army, but he knew that once you retreated from disputed turf it was tough to fight your way back. So he gave her his best smile, and it was usually pretty effective with women. "I'm sure it's a simple clerical error." He picked up the room phone before she could argue any more and asked for the manager to come up.

Fortunately, they didn't have long to wait. The woman continued cutting tags off clothes, using a small, curved pair of nail scissors that clicked with annoyance.

They stayed like that, she snipping tags and he standing by the phone until a soft knock was heard. When he answered, a corporate-looking type in his fifties stood there with a bland, practiced, everything-will-be-fine smile. "How can we help you, sir?"

The manager's smile wilted like week-old lettuce when the woman stepped up and yanked the door wide. "You seem to have booked both of us into the same room. I think we have a problem."

And she was right. The manager, two front desk clerks and the computer all confirmed what he'd known from the moment that woman screamed. He and the lady in blue pajamas were both booked into the very last room in the hotel. ·

"But that's impossible," Emily argued. Emily Saunders, that was her name; he'd found out as they went through the bookings. "I can't share a room with a strange man."

"I'm not that strange once you get to know me," he assured her.

She sent him a glance that suggested she didn't find this setup remotely funny.

"I am very sorry, Ms. Saunders. There are simply no more rooms."

"But I booked a single room. In advance."

"Me, too," he interjected.

"Naturally, your money will be refunded in full," he promised them smoothly, which didn't exactly solve the problem.

"What about the lobby?" she cried. "Isn't there a cot, or a sofa or something he could sleep on?"

"All the cots are in use. And, as you'll recall, we only have wing chairs in the lobby."

"A sleeping bag on the floor, then."

Jonah was a pretty easygoing guy, but this was going too far. He had his team to think of. "I have an important day tomorrow," he told her. "I need my sleep. You bed down on the lobby floor."

She stalked right up to him, nose to his collarbone. Their lack of equality in the height department seemed to aggravate her even more. "I have an important day tomorrow, too."

"I'm competing in a hockey tournament."

"I'm a bridesmaid in a wedding."

"My condolences."

The way her eyes suddenly widened, he got the odd feeling she agreed with his assessment of being stuck in a wedding party. "But this is ridiculous. There must be somewhere else you could stay."

He'd booked the hotel for a reason. He was too old to bunk in with a bunch of hockey players trading war stories and shooting the bull. Most of the others were too old for it, too, but it didn't stop them. He thought with wives and kids at home, they needed the male bonding time a lot more than he did. At this point, he'd rather sleep on the floor of the Elk Crossing Lodge's lobby than on the floor of a cabin with six guys, at least half of whom were bound to snore. But he'd much rather sleep in a nice comfortable bed right here in this room.

"There isn't anybody else I can stay with. What about you? Can't you stay with somebody else from the wedding?"

She blinked at him once, slowly, and then shook her head sharply. "Impossible."

He shrugged. "It's not ideal, but we'll just have to share for a night or two. There are two beds. I don't snore."

She crossed her hands under her breasts and he tried not to notice. "It's not your snoring that worries me."

"I don't have evil designs on your body, either," he said, trying to reassure her of his integrity. She was a good-looking woman and if they'd both stumbled into this hotel room in passion it would be one thing, but that wasn't the case.

If he could get her to see him as a platonic room-mate, they'd be fine. "Look—" he indicated the hockey stick leaning against the wall "—I'm playing two, three games a day. I'll only be in the room to sleep, and too tired even to think about women."

She raised one eyebrow as though finding that hard to believe, as indeed it was. He could probably be dead and still think about women. So he pulled his trump card. "You can trust me. I'm a cop."

She seemed less than impressed by this display of trustworthiness. "What are you going to do? Arrest the bedbugs?"

"Thought I might shoot them." For a second her mouth softened and she almost smiled, then caught herself.

She turned back to the doorway.

"Are you telling me there is absolutely no way you can force this man to leave my room?" she snapped at the three uniforms hovering nervously near the door.

The hotel manager took a deep breath. "The computer was malfunctioning and you were both given the same room. Unless one of you is willing to leave..." The manager glanced from one to the other, but they both held their ground. "I'm so sorry."

"Can you at least tell me when I'll have my clothes back?"

"As soon as possible. We've put a rush on everything."

She turned back to him, her hair swinging in a silky curtain. "I carry mace. I'll be sleeping with it under my pillow."

"Hey, it's got to be better to share a room with me than bedbugs."

"Don't flatter yourself."

3

HAVING HER MINIMAL NEW wardrobe organized, Emily got out the nail polish. Tomorrow, the paper rose making continued, then, most of the out-of-town guests would have arrived so there was a big potluck dinner.

Even though Emily hadn't grown up here, she'd spent a lot of time in Elk Crossing as a kid, because so much of her family still lived in the area. It was going to be quite the reunion.

It had been a weird day already, now she was supposed to share a room with a big, smelly hockey player?

She tried to ignore him as he schlepped his big, stupid hockey bag over to his side of the room. At least he was taking the bed beside the curtain, leaving her with the one closest to the door and the bathroom.

Once he'd settled himself, he said, "There's no mini-bar or fridge."

"No. They don't rent the room, remember?"

He grunted and went out of the room, sadly not taking his belongings with him, only to return a minute later with a bucket of ice.

He unzipped his monstrously large sports bag and dug out a six-pack of Budweiser beer. Perhaps he felt the force of her gaze on him, because he glanced up.

His eyes were blue and twinkled as if he thought this whole thing was a great joke.

He pulled a can out of the plastic holder. Held it aloft with his eyebrows raised. "Wanna beer?"

He gave her his beefcake calendar grin, as though he thought she might have missed it the first time he flashed it.

She figured they might as well try to get along since they were stuck here together, so she nodded. To her surprise he got up and brought her over the can, even popping the top when she looked helplessly at her wet nails. "Glass?"

"No, thanks."

He nodded and went back to his bed. Stacked the pillows behind him and popped his own beer.

"Are you really a cop?"

For answer, he lifted his butt and dragged out his cop badge. She rose and went for a closer look. The badge told her that he was, indeed, a cop, and he was from Oregon.

"Sergeant Jonah Betts," she read aloud.

He held out his hand. "Pleased to meet you, Emily Saunders."

It was so ridiculous she had to chuckle. "Likewise." They shook hands. He didn't do the he-man squish-all-her-bones thing, but it was still a firm clasp. His hands were big and warm, but she noticed he was careful not to mess up her still-damp nails.

"Most people call me Emily."

"So, how was your day, Emily?"

She returned to her seat at the desk and carefully painted her baby fingernail while she replied. "This has been a very strange day. Apart from the obvious bedbug thing, this morning. Let's see, I went to Wal-Mart wearing clothes I would rather not have been seen in."

He nodded, understanding. "I remember. I'm guessing that's not your normal look."

"No. So naturally I bumped into someone I sort of knew years ago, a big mouth who happens to be friends with my cousin who's getting married." Carefully re-screwing the lid on the polish, she blew on her finger-tips. "She saw me in the lovely outfit I was wearing, buying fashion at Wal-Mart and couldn't keep the story to herself. At the lunch today? My dad offered me a business loan, my mom said she could help me with the cost of the bridesmaid gown and my aunt tells me she's going to set me up with my third cousin Buddy, the or-thodontist."

"Why didn't you tell the nosy broad about the bedbugs?"

"I am staying in this hotel in order to avoid being billeted in a family room somewhere, either on a pullout couch or an air mattress. My family does big weddings, so I wouldn't have the family room to myself, you understand. It would be like a weeklong slumber party on really bad mattresses with people I barely know."

"So you chose me, instead."

"You wouldn't be so flattered if you knew my family." She blew out a breath. "I'm sure there will be people checking out tomorrow and I'll get another room. Once I'm in that family room? I'm stuck for the week."

"What kind of business do you have?"

"I'm a massage therapist. I run a wellness clinic. We have naturopaths, a chiropractor, a nutritionist and a

practitioner of traditional Chinese medicine all on staff.
We work as an integrated team."

"Cool," he said, though from his tone she guessed
he wasn't a big believer in alternative medicine.

"I enjoy it."

"And, I'm guessing from the fact that they want to
set you up with Cousin Buddy the orthodontist, that
you're single?"

"And loving it," she informed him. After a day of
pity for her spinster state, she was feeling militant.

He put up his hands, so fast she heard the beer slosh
in the can. "Hey, I'm single, too. I get it."

She looked at him curiously. Did the same unsubtle
hints happen with men, too? "Do your family try to
match you up with someone every chance they get?"

He sipped beer while thinking it over. Nodded. "My
friends more. I'm the last one of my buddies still a free
man. They see me as a challenge, but I aim to stay
single."

She raised her beer can in a toast. "To freedom."

The both drank. "You want to watch some TV?"

"Sure." Anything that would take her mind off the
week ahead would be good.

While she applied a second coat of polish, he found
the remote and punched channels. She heard him skip
over some kind of cop show, make a rude remark about
Dancing with the Stars, and then she heard the buzz of
a news station. That she could live with. She was
moving to her bed so she could see the TV when there
was a knock on the door.

"Now what?"

"Do you mind?" She was closer to the door, but her
polish was wet. "Maybe they've found another room."

He rolled off the bed and padded to the door.

Opened it.

"Did you order an orange tent?" he asked, staring in some disbelief at the dress hanging from a chamber-maid's hand.

"My dress," she cried, getting up. "Is it okay?" she asked the woman.

"Yes. We hung it in the big freezer. It's what the ex-terminators told us to do. Anything that was on there will be dead by now."

"Too bad that dress isn't," said Jonah.

THERE WERE SO MANY PEOPLE in town for the wedding that the potluck dinner that night was held in the Masonic Hall, where the wedding reception was also booked. Emily knew that in the next couple of days she'd spend many hours helping decorate the gym-nasium-size space into what her aunt Irene insisted on calling the bower of bliss.

As an out-of-towner, Emily wasn't expected to bring food, but she stopped at the deli anyhow and picked up a tub of potato salad. She'd have taken wine, but Uncle Bill had told her proudly he'd made enough for the entire week. Uncle Bill was a good man and one of her favorite relatives, but she'd rather use his wine as nail polish remover than drink the stuff.

As she walked in, her aunt rushed up to her. "Oh, Emily, I'm so glad you're here. Cousin Buddy is dying to meet you." She took the offered potato salad and dropped her voice, explaining, "He's the one I was telling you about. Very successful. An orthodontist."

She made flappy come-here motions with her hand to a guy standing with Emily's mom and dad. Her folks immediately shooed him her way, acting in unison, so they looked like a vaudeville act. *Yep,* Emily thought, *my family haven't lost any of their subtlety.*

She hadn't had high hopes of an orthodontist in his thirties who went by the name Buddy, and she wasn't disappointed. Her third cousin sauntered over looking at her with an expression that said, "Ta-da, it's your lucky day." He was of medium height with wispy blond hair and round, steel-rimmed spectacles, behind which pale blue eyes took in the world with a self-satisfied air.

"Emily, this is Cousin Buddy." Honestly, the way she said it, Emily could hear the unspoken, *she's single, too!*

"Hello," she said, extending her hand at the same time Buddy leaned in for a kiss. She turned her head so his lips landed on her cheek, leaving a wet print that felt as if a dog had licked her face.

"Well, I'll leave you two to get to know each other," Aunt Irene said and scuttled off, sending her mom and dad a double thumbs-up.

Buddy was probably a perfectly nice guy, she told herself, and he was family. So, she put a pleasant smile on her face, pretended not to notice that her nearest and dearest were watching her and Cousin Buddy as though they were acting out the season-ending cliff-hanger of a particularly juicy and addictive soap opera. "I haven't seen you at any family weddings before," she said for something to say.

"No. I've always been too occupied with my practice and busy social life. But a man gets to a certain stage in life where he starts to appreciate the importance of family. And I had a couple of weeks with nothing to do so I thought I'd hang out and see folks I haven't seen since I was a kid."

"That's nice." But did he have to stand in her personal space?

"Who wants wine?" Uncle Bill strolled up with a tray of filled glasses. "The white's a chardonnay and the red's an infidel."

"Thanks," Buddy said, reaching for a glass of red.

"Maybe later," she told Uncle Bill.

Buddy took a sip of wine and when his eyes didn't water she said, "I think he meant Zinfandel, but I wouldn't be too sure. Uncle Bill's wine is pretty strong."

Buddy sent her a lecherous glance. "I like my booze like I like my women. Strong and tasty."

Oh, boy.

"Leanne," she called desperately to the woman walking by. "How's the bride?"

"Hey, Em. Oh, good, you met Buddy. Come sit with us."

"Great." So she followed her cousin to one of the long tables and Buddy followed.

Leanne was probably her favorite cousin, apart from her taste in bridesmaid dresses, and she seemed to have found the perfect man for her. Derek was an accounting major she'd met in college, obviously crazy about his soon-to-be wife, and the kind of man you could call on when you got a flat tire in the middle of the night. They were planning to put down roots in Elk Crossing, where Leanne already had a job teaching kindergarten.

Their table was made up mostly of the bridal party and their friends, so it was a young bunch, getting raucous as they chugged down Uncle Bill's wine. Emily, from bitter experience, stuck to water, as did Leanne.

Buddy spent most of the dinner bragging about his practice, his shrewd investments and even, for ten interminable minutes, reminiscing about each and every expensive car he'd ever owned. Meanwhile, he was putting back a lot of Uncle Bill's wine, which she was pretty sure had an alcohol content that would rival Screech rum.

On Emily's other side was a woman in her early twenties who was a friend of Leanne's. Emily had met Kirsten Rempel a few times and liked her a lot. She was pretty, fun and smart, but she'd had some bad career luck. A cute blonde with lots of energy, Kirsten had moved to Elk Crossing to work in promotions at the local radio station. Unfortunately, she relocated for the job before discovering that the radio station manager was a sexist boor. She'd lasted three months, and since then had been making her living as a hostess and server at one of two upscale restaurants in town.

Everyone had expected her to move on, but she seemed to have got stuck in this town. Now she was waitressing to bring in some money and dating a guy nobody thought was good enough for her. He also had a bad habit of letting her down, like tonight, so she was here alone.

Emily was happy to have Kirsten to talk to since it gave her a break from Buddy.

"How are things?"

"Good." Her blond hair swung as Kirsten leaned forward. "The restaurant's okay, but I need to find something else." There was something about the way she spoke that made Emily wonder if she'd still be giving the same speech ten years from now. It happened to people sometimes in Elk Crossing. They came here and sort of got pulled into the town and couldn't seem to get it together to move on.

She almost wished she'd had some of Uncle Bill's "wine" so she'd have the courage to give this woman she barely knew a little pep talk. Not only was she in a dead end job but even Emily, who didn't live here, knew her so-called boyfriend was far from faithful. And given that Kirsten was far too good for him, it drove her crazy.

Somebody challenged Derek to a drinking game and Kirsten cried, "No, they should play *Newlywed Game*."

Then she put on her radio announcer's voice, her whole body coming to life as she got into her role. "Now, Derek and Leanne, you'll be asked a series of questions about each other. We'll be able to tell if you're truly compatible, if your love is the real thing, if your marriage will last, based on how much you know—or think you know—about each other."

A great deal of laughter and hooting accompanied the questions Kirsten came up with. "What is Derek's favorite kitchen appliance, and why?"

Naturally, Leanne had lots of help answering the question. "The vibrator is not a kitchen appliance, Don," Kirsten reminded Derek's friend. "You're disqualified."

"She keeps it in her kitchen!" he yelled. "I've seen it."

"That was my cream whipper," Leanne insisted, very red in the face.

"Okay, okay," Kirsten said when the catcalls had died down. "Here's a serious question and no one but Derek can answer. What's Leanne's favorite movie?"

"Star Wars," he proclaimed.

There was a burst of laughter. "That's *your* favorite movie," Leanne reminded him.

"I thought it was yours, too."

"Nope."

"What is it, then?"

"Gone with the Wind."

Derek was incensed. "You can't say *Gone with the Wind*. Every chick says her favorite movie is *Gone with the Wind*. It's like not having an opinion at all."

"Except that it really is my favorite movie. Vivien Leigh and Clark Gable? When he carries her up the stairs?" She sighed gustily, all the women at the table nodding in agreement. "Are you kidding me? You don't see movies like that anymore."

"Know what my favorite movie is?" Buddy asked loudly, not seeming to realize the question-and-answer game was restricted to the bridal couple.

"What?"

"21."

Derek said, "Isn't that the one about those MIT kids who clean up in Vegas?"

"Yep. It's based on a true story. These kids invented a system to win at the casinos using math. Brilliant."

"So, you're a gambler?" Leanne asked.

He shrugged. "I think above-average intelligence allows certain people to achieve above-average returns. I don't call that gambling." He slurred a little over his words.

"How about you, Emily?" Derek wanted to know. "What's your favorite movie?" She couldn't help wondering if Derek was trying to pull her and Buddy into some kind of compatibility game. If so, she'd happily prove that she and the money-obsessed dentist couldn't be more different.

"My favorite movie is *Wall Street.* It's about how greed destroys people." She smiled demurely and sipped her water.

Leanne pulled her aside, ostensibly to discuss bridal matters. "*Wall Street?* What is the matter with you? *Sense and Sensibility* is your favorite movie."

"Buddy's getting on my last nerve. All he's interested in is money. Who cares about his Mercedes Coupe? There's more to life."

Leanne sighed. "He's trying to impress you. I bet he's a really nice guy once you get to know him."

"But not my type."

"I only want to see you as happy as I am with Derek." She gave Emily a quick hug. "We all do."

"I know. And please don't remind me I'm not getting any younger because your mom and mine already tag-teamed me on that one. Thirty-one is not exactly ancient. I'm picky, that's all."

"I know."

Unfortunately, Buddy hadn't listened when she'd tried to tell him that Uncle Bill's homemade wine was about four hundred percent pure alcohol. Leanne had made her feel a little bad so she went and got him a coffee to go with his tiramisu. He ignored both and downed more of the red hooch, moving his chair closer to hers and slurring in her ear. Buddy was becoming an annoying drunk. The sooner he passed out the happier she'd be.

But he didn't pass out. He got…amorous.

He moved his chair even closer so their knees butted against each other. She moved hers farther away so

Kirsten could be forgiven for thinking she was making a pass.

He put an arm around her, big and overwarm. She was sure she could feel his sweat through the wool of his jacket.

She shifted so the arm fell off her and next thing his hand was on her thigh, making her thankful her temporary wardrobe was all wash and wear.

Finally, obviously realizing he was being too subtle, he said to her, "Let's you and me get out of here."

"I don't think so."

"Come on, I want to show you something."

"I'm pretty sure I don't want to see it."

He giggled. "You're cute. Mature, I like that in a woman."

She glanced around with "help me" blazing from her eyes. No one seemed to notice or thought about rescuing her. No one. Leanne was too busy being in love with Derek, Kirsten was on her cell phone, presumably tracking down the whereabouts of her loser boyfriend, and everybody else was busy with their own affairs. Everyone except for her mother and father, who were watching Buddy hit on her with hope shining in their faces.

"I really have to go now," she said at last to Buddy. "I've got a headache." Maybe it was rude to leave so early, but she had had enough. Perhaps because she was inherently polite, or maybe because her parents were watching, she added, "It was nice meeting y—"

Her words were cut off by his mouth. His big, sloppy, wet, bad-red-wine-tasting mouth. He kissed her as though she were an air mattress he was trying to blow up in a hurry. He fastened his mouth on to hers, creating an air lock. When she grabbed his shoulders and yanked her face away she was sure she heard a pop.

Outraged, she looked around for her protective family to come and deal with this drunken moron. She caught her parents exchanging a high five, and her aunt smiling broadly, already taking credit for the match.

She jumped to her feet and headed for the exit, too fast for anyone to catch up with her. On the way she pulled a tissue from her bag and wiped her mouth. Yuck.

4

"HI, HONEY. YOU'RE HOME EARLY," a gravelly voice said when she threw open the door to 318 a short time later. "Did you have a good time?"

"Don't even get me started."

Jonah glanced up from the hockey game he was watching on television. "Wow, you look mad. What happened?"

"Cousin Buddy happened. He got drunk and hit on me and—" Unable to adequately describe how gross the entire escapade had been, she said, "Eeew."

"Got it. Want a beer?"

"Desperately."

He popped the top of one and handed her a cold can.

"Thanks." She took a grateful swig, hoping it would erase Buddy's taste. "Why are you here? I thought you were boozing with the boys tonight."

He pointed to his leg and she now saw the ice pack wrapped around his thigh.

"Uh-oh."

"Yeah. I pulled something. Hurts like a bitch."

"How long have you had the ice pack on?"

"I don't know." He squinted at the clock. "Forty minutes or so?"

"Take it off. Give it a rest."

"Can you do anything for me? In a professional capacity?"

"Depends. If you've torn the muscle, then no. If it's in spasm, then yes. You want me to have a look?"

He nodded.

The room phone rang. Jonah leaned over and answered it. "Yeah?" A pause. Then he glanced up at her, looking sheepish. "No, you got the right room. She's right here."

He passed her the phone.

"Hello?"

"Who was that?" Leanne asked her.

Damn. "Why didn't you call my cell? You always call my cell."

"I had to lend Derek my phone since his died. I'm at my mom's and I couldn't remember your cell number so I called the hotel." Her voice grew low and intimate. "I guess you're busted. Was that Buddy? Did I interrupt something?"

"No! It's not Buddy. He is a disgusting drunk, only interested in his fabulous cars and amazing stock picks. Did I tell you what he told me about his portfolio?" She thought if she babbled on enough about Buddy she could get Leanne to forget about the man who had answered the phone in her hotel room.

Her plan didn't work.

"If that's not Buddy in your room, then who is it?"

"It's…well, it's kind of complicated," she started, trying to think of something fast, words that would explain a strange man answering her phone, while at the same time not including the word *bedbugs* or making her seem like a skank. Seconds passed.

"I'm listening."

"His name is Jonah."

"Nice name. And?"

"And, he's…" Jonah was looking half guilty, half amused as she stumbled her way through half phrases. "He's—" *What?* Why was it that whenever she needed to think fast on her feet her brain froze over. Only one idea came to her and once it had lodged in her brain nothing better came along. "He's…my boyfriend," she ended in a rush.

She didn't know who was more surprised when the words came out of her mouth, her or Jonah.

Or Leanne.

"Your boyfriend?"

"Yes." She turned her body slightly so she was no longer looking at her brand-new boyfriend. "His name is Jonah."

"You already told me his name. What I want to know is if you have a boyfriend in town why you never said anything. How come he wasn't at dinner tonight?"

"It's sort of complicated." She tapped her nails on the beer can wondering how she could possibly have come up with such a ridiculous story. "He's in town for the hockey tournament, so he couldn't come tonight."

"And you never told me about him because…?"

She felt her cheeks beginning to heat. She really wished her unwanted roomie would go somewhere else for five minutes and give her some privacy, but he'd even muted the TV so he could eavesdrop better. He seemed as fascinated by her halting explanation about him being her boyfriend as Leanne was.

"I guess I didn't want to share him." Now that she'd settled on an explanation, it was easier to embellish. She could absolutely see herself hiding a boyfriend from her family—if she actually had a boyfriend. "You know what the family's like. Dad would be asking him his intentions and Mom would be pricing wedding invitations and Aunt Alice would probably grill him on his sperm count." A choke sounded behind her. "That's why I keep my private life private."

"Wow. You could have told me, though." Leanne sounded a little hurt. "How long have you two been going out?"

"Not long." In fact, she could count her relationship in minutes.

"You left so early tonight, I was worried about you. Now I know why."

"Yeah. You know how it is at the beginning of a relationship."

In her peripheral vision she noticed Jonah settle back against his stacked pillows, obviously enjoying her predicament hugely. A certain speculation in his eyes.

Leanne sighed, the sigh of a true romantic. "You mean when you think about them all the time and can't wait to be together? When you think about sex all the time?"

"Uh-huh," she agreed weakly. "All the time."

"How is the sex?"

The whole situation was so ridiculous, with Leanne rhapsodizing about her made-up love life and Jonah doing his best to listen to every word, that she found herself giggling. She turned to Jonah and said aloud, "My cousin wants to know how the sex is?"

His grin was instant and wolfish. The way he looked at her made her suddenly realize it was not smart to tease a wolf. "Tell her it's fantastic."

She rolled her eyes. Leanne was cracking up on the

other end of the phone. "I definitely want to meet this guy, when you're not too busy having fantastic sex."

"I'm sure you will."

"I'll meet him at the wedding, anyway, right?"

"Um, it depends on his hockey schedule."

"No way. He has to come. Tell him."

"Okay."

"Now. Or put me on the phone and I'll tell him."

She held the phone away from her ear once again, and wished she was home in Portland in her pajamas watching a chick flick on DVD. Anything but this.

Since it was his fault for answering in the first place, she held out the phone to him and smiled sweetly. "Leanne wants to make sure you're coming to the wedding."

JONAH ALMOST FORGOT THE PAIN in his thigh watching his roomie trying to explain why a man was answering her room phone. He'd never seen a more incompetent liar. And hadn't she dropped herself right in it?

"You can stop smirking," she snapped when she got off the phone. "This is your fault."

He leaned back against his pillows, his gaze never leaving her face. Cute face, kind of flushed right now, and her lips seemed a little plumper. Maybe they were like Pinocchio's nose. When she told a lie they plumped up. Or maybe it was talking about sex that did it.

"So, I'm your boyfriend, huh?"

"I'm sorry. It was all I could think of."

"It's not so bad," he said, thinking. "Should keep Buddy the orthodontist out of your mouth."

She groaned. "That is a horrible pun. And you don't know my family. They'll want to meet you."

He heard the panic in her tone. "Am I so terrible?"

"No. Of course not." She looked at him dispassionately. "If you shaved and wore decent clothes, you'd be perfectly presentable. But they have this charming quality where if you get to thirty and are still single they panic and try to marry you off. To anybody."

"Right. But look at the good side. I can be your beard. You don't want to get married, I don't want to get married. We're not really a couple, so nobody's going to get pressured into anything."

"You don't seem very upset about being stuck with an instant girlfriend." She was nibbling on that pouty lower lip now, a job, he realized, he'd gladly take over. You got to know a person pretty fast when you shared a confined space with them, and he was starting to like this person in the next bed. Even though it was his fault for answering the hotel phone, she seemed to feel guilty for lying about their relationship.

"I can see certain benefits," he said, settling back.

Her eyes instantly narrowed and she released her lip from between her teeth.

"Not those benefits," he told her. "I was thinking that if I agree to show up to the wedding, you might take pity on me and give me a massage—" he looked at her "—or two."

And, because she still seemed a little skittish, he added, "Emily, I'm going to make you a promise. I won't make a pass at you."

She didn't exactly look relieved. It was a big deal for him to promise to keep his hands off a desirable woman who happened to be sharing his hotel room. Instead of looking grateful she seemed—pissed off. He couldn't imagine she felt insulted. She was gorgeous.

Men must make fools of themselves all the time over her. But since he was the first person to admit he didn't have a clue about women, he continued.

"You're beautiful. And under normal circumstances, I'd be doing my level best to get you into my hotel room. But since you're here against your will, I give you my word I won't try anything."

She picked up a brand-new set of sweats and disappeared into the bathroom. When she returned, she was wearing the gray fleece, and she'd also gathered a couple of towels and a bottle of some kind of oil.

He was doing his best to concentrate on CNN and not the fact that sometimes his principles really got in the way of his sex life, when she came toward him. She said, "So, you're saying there's no way you and I would ever have sex."

"No." She was so sexy he wished he'd kept his mouth shut. A woman walking toward him with a bottle of massage oil and he'd announced he wasn't going to touch her? He must be a mental case. "I said I wouldn't hit on you."

She settled beside him on the bed, shifting his leg so she could spread the towel underneath him. "Isn't that the same thing?"

"Not at all." When she was this close he could smell her skin and see that her eyes weren't completely brown as he'd thought. There were flecks of gold and tiny slivers of green in them, as well. As she settled her hands above his knee and began to gently probe the muscle, he said, "I'm giving you an open invitation to hit on me."

Her fingers stalled and her eyes widened.

He grinned up at her. "Anytime."

5

DAY THREE OF LEANNE AND DEREK'S Wedding Week Extravaganza was almost done, Emily thought with relief as she sat quietly at the desk in her hotel room, blessedly alone, writing out place cards for the wedding.

Today she'd had lunch with her mom. She loved her mom, but the "nice, long lunch, just the two of us," had been somewhat marred by her mother's enthusiastic comments about Cousin Buddy and her wistful excitement about Leanne's wedding.

Emily successfully navigated the conversation around dangerous spots, like how lucky Leanne and Derek were to have found each other when they were both so young, interspersed with hints about how it got more and more difficult to find a mate as you got older and more set in your ways.

Naturally, this led to the story of crazy Aunt Hilda who never married and ended up living on a rotting houseboat with nothing but seven cats for company. "All she ever bought was cat food. I'm not saying Hilda was eating it, but you have to wonder." She shook her head. Did she really think Emily had never heard this story before? "At least she didn't have to worry about mice."

They made it all the way to coffee, when her carefully steered conversation hit a Titanic iceberg. Her mother's eyes filled and she said, "You know I love Leanne and I'm truly happy for her, and for Irene. But if my sister gets to be a grandmother first, I'll just die."

She'd spent the rest of the day feeling guilty somehow and that she had to make it up to her mom, which meant she'd ended up volunteering to do the place cards. Maybe her mom couldn't boast of a happily married, eagerly breeding daughter, but she could damn well be proud of having such a helpful one.

Her silence was rudely interrupted by the door opening followed by a series of crashes.

"What are you doing?" The unholy racket caused her to turn her head and see Jonah stumble in with a whole lot of hockey equipment hanging off him.

"Sorry, I was trying to be quiet." He banged the door behind him and some sort of pad tumbled to the floor. When he bent to reach it, two hockey sticks banged on the wall.

"It's like Marley's ghost entering the room."

"Looks like rain. I didn't want to leave anything in the truck to get damp."

"Great. This hotel room isn't nearly crowded enough. What it needed was more hockey equipment."

As one, they both glanced at the big orange pouf of a dress hanging from the outside of the closet because, just as in her first room, there simply wasn't room to cram all that dress inside.

The dress cast a faintly orange glow over everything, she was convinced. It definitely affected her mood.

He looked doubtfully beyond his bed. "I could put

the stuff behind that curtain, but it's probably damper there than in my truck."

"Don't mind me. I'm feeling bitchy. No idea why."

He hefted the sticks, bag, padding, two pairs of skates and a uniform over to his bed and settled it in an untidy pile. He grunted as he yanked the liners out of his skates and placed them in front of the radiator as he had the night before.

She turned back to her task. No wonder she was thinking of Marley's ghost; her current task was positively Dickensian.

She tried to ignore the unmistakable sounds of a man undressing by focusing all her attention on the nib of her pen.

"Okay if I take a shower now?" the deep voice asked.

"Yes. Fine."

He passed behind and she felt him pause. "What are you doing?"

"Calligraphy."

"I know what it is," he said, surprising her. "What I meant is, why are you doing it now?"

"I'm writing out the place cards for the wedding," she said, carefully finishing the *Y* on *Cathy* and double-checking the spelling of Cathy's last name from the list beside the neat stack of cards.

"They had to get an out-of-town guest to do those? A couple days before the wedding?"

She put down her pen and turned. "Obviously, you've never been a bridesmaid." She wished she hadn't turned. She found herself at eye level with his scrumptious abs and the waistband of his gray sweatpants. She could smell him. He smelled athletic, of clean sweat and hard work. If she ran her hands over his body his muscles would still be warm and pliable from exertion.

"Good guess." He sounded amused. Again.

"It's part of my responsibility to help with all the little details that may have been overlooked." She glanced at the stack of cards waiting to be painstakingly written, and lied through her teeth, "I really don't mind."

"I'm sure you've got better things to do."

"Honestly? I'm missing another potluck dinner. And the choosing of the embarrassing baby and child photos to be shown on the projector at the reception. Frankly, I prefer this job."

"As soon as I'm cleaned up, I'm meeting a few of the guys for a pizza. You want to join us?"

She was genuinely surprised by the offer. And she smiled her thanks at him. "Thank you. But if I don't keep going, I'll never get these done. Besides, I've got a yogurt and a couple of granola bars if I get hungry. I'll be fine."

"Suit yourself." Then he ambled into the bathroom and soon she heard the shower running.

Three place cards later, he was out again, freshly shaved and smelling of soap and shampoo. In her peripheral vision she noted he was wearing nothing but a towel, and that the hair of his lower legs was dark and his big feet were leaving damp prints on the carpet.

When he was past her, she allowed herself a quick glance at his back view, on the grounds that a hardworking calligrapher needed a little treat now and then. She was happy to note that his hairiness didn't go as far as his back. That was smooth of skin and heavy with muscle. This guy did more than play hockey to stay in shape. Her professional eye noted that his right deltoid was more developed than his left. He was definitely right-handed.

If he were her patient she'd encourage him to put some effort into developing the muscles on his left side, simply to even him out and balance the stress on his spine. But he wasn't her patient and she had cards to inscribe.

Although, she supposed he was a sort of patient. "How's your quad holding up?"

"I did the stretching like you told me. It's not too bad today."

"Good. Keep doing the stretches. At least three times a day."

"Yes, Doc."

Two more minutes and he was heading back out the door. "Sure you won't change your mind?"

"No. But you have fun."

"See you later." And he was gone.

She carefully crossed off a name and continued to the next, trying not to let resentment get the better of her. Maybe she'd have liked to go for pizza with a bunch of hockey players. Doubtful, but maybe she'd have liked to go for a run or see a movie, dance naked in the rain.

However, she could do none of those things so long as she was chained to this desk on calligraphy duty.

"You have such a neat hand," her aunt had gushed, as she handed over the job.

Years of practice, was her silent answer.

"Emily's such a help," her mother agreed. "So reliable."

Maybe she was sick of being reliable. The notion of tossing the entire stack of cards into the wastepaper basket brought a momentary smile to her face, but of course she'd never do anything like that, so she stretched her cramped fingers and went back to work, the room quiet but for the scratching sound of the pen nib on the card stock.

And that's exactly how Jonah found her two hours later.

The door opened with a tremendous crash. She'd have assumed it meant he was drunk, but she was beginning to realize that Jonah was simply a noisy person. There was nothing he did that he didn't do at maximum volume. "You still at it?" Even his voice sounded unnecessarily loud in the previously quiet room.

"Only ten more to go."

She became aware that the most amazing smell had entered the room along with her roommate. Her mouth started watering almost before her conscious mind registered the source of the smell.

She turned and found him holding out a square pizza box. "For you."

If he'd brought her roses—no, diamonds—she couldn't have felt more grateful.

"I have never been so happy to see anything in my life," she sighed. Then squeaked a protest as he tried to place the thing on the desktop. "No! I can't get grease on those place cards. Put it on the bed." She glanced at her fingers, smudged with ink. "I'll go wash up and be right back."

When she returned he'd opened her a beer and placed it on the bedside table along with the pizza box.

She used a hand towel from the bathroom as a napkin and opened the box. Her stomach growled.

"I wasn't sure what you like so I got the works."

"Perfect." She lifted her first slice, trailing a wonderful, delicious, stretchy strand of cheese all the way to her mouth. She bit down and all the flavors exploded at once. Cheese and garlic, tomato sauce, mushroom, some kind of ham, a sliver of green pepper. "Oh, mmm. Mmm." She moaned with pleasure and caught him staring at her mouth. For a second the connection scorched, then he abruptly looked away, grabbed his own beer and took a drink.

"How did your games go today?" she asked him, mostly since it was the first thing she could think of to say that would break the strange atmosphere.

"We played two. One easy win, one tough. And I watched a couple. Some good games."

"That's good."

"How about you? Apart from slaving like a medieval monk on your calligraphy, what did you do today?"

"We went shopping and got some stuff for Leanne's stagette party tomorrow night. Had lunch with the girls and hung out."

"Good times."

"Yeah."

Because the pizza was far too much for her to eat alone she offered him half and was only mildly surprised when he scarfed the slices as though he hadn't already eaten.

"I can't believe you can eat two dinners and not get fat," she complained.

"That wasn't a dinner," he exclaimed, "that was a little before-bed snack." He settled back with the last piece of pizza and said, "Besides, I have a fast metabolism."

She wiped her fingers and folded the empty box into the trash. Then she washed her hands with hot water and soap, all the way up to her elbows like a surgeon, drying herself thoroughly. When she came back out of the bathroom she said, "I'm going to finish these last ten cards before I turn in."

"Okay. I'll watch some TV."

Soon they were absorbed in their respective activities. She was crossing the *T* on *Patricia* with a flourish when a loud sound, like a sudden rattle of stones against a window, startled her so much she scraped her pen, leaving a destructive trail of black ink that pretty much crossed out *Patricia*.

She raised her head. The sound came again, louder now and more persistent, like steel drums. It sounded like street drummers, each with their own rhythm, had set up inside her hotel room.

"What on earth?"

Jonah muted the television. With a grimace he said, "I told you it looked like rain." Then he pulled the curtain back and she saw the drops of water already plopping down from the leaking roof to hit the buckets, each drop of rain making a piercing noise.

"Oh, no. I don't believe it."

She liked the sound of rain on a roof, she really did. The sound was rhythmic, lulling almost; it reminded her of being curled up in bed as a youngster with a good book, dry and warm.

But she'd never tried to snuggle up in bed with that same rain falling through the roof into plastic buckets that echoed.

There was no lulling rhythm, just constant scatters of sharp sound. Over and over again.

"How long does rain tend to last in these parts?" he asked conversationally.

"It can go on for days." She glanced at the curtain. "And nights."

She managed to finish the cards, then brushed her teeth, donned her pajamas in the bathroom and returned to the room, feeling much less self-conscious than she had the night before. Already she was getting used to Jonah. How odd.

He used the bathroom after her, and trod past her wearing the shorts she strongly suspected he'd donned for her benefit.

They settled in their respective beds and after politely checking with him, she flipped off the light.

The room was plunged into relative darkness, which had the effect of making the staccato rain splashing into the plastic buckets sound even louder.

She turned her back to the curtain, shoved a pillow over her ear and resolutely shut her eyes. Now it sounded like the entire cast of *Stomp* performing. Only without any discernable rhythm.

She flipped to her other side and tried blocking the other ear. It made no difference. At least she knew her hearing was the same in both ears.

She flopped to her back, contemplated the darkness above her, where the timber beams of the roof protected them from the weather, and hoped very much that the leak didn't spread to her part of the room.

She could tell from his breathing and restless movements that Jonah wasn't having any better luck than she falling asleep.

Finally, she said, "Jonah?"

"Yeah?"

"Are you sleepy?"

A low chuckle answered her. "Not a chance. It's too much like being under fire."

Her eyes widened and she turned to where he was no more than a gray outline. "Have you ever been?"

"Under fire? I've been a cop for a dozen years. Of course I have."

"Did you ever—" She stopped herself. "Never mind."

She heard the movement of his head against his pillow, knew he was looking her way. "Kill anyone?" He waited a beat and she didn't answer. "That's what you wanted to know, isn't it? Everyone wonders. I guess it's natural. No. Thank God. I almost did once, but my aim was off and the guy was coming at me too fast." He sounded so matter-of-fact, but the image in her mind was terrifying. "We both fired at the same time. I got him in the right chest. Broke a rib and he lost some blood, but he was okay. His bullet hit me in the left arm. Which left me with a manly and interesting scar. Someday I'll show you."

A tiny shiver went through her at his words. Obviously, if she wanted to look, she could see the scar on one of the occasions when he sauntered past her in nothing but a towel or his running shorts, but the idea of him actually showing her his wound sounded vaguely intimate. And she had no idea how to respond. *Thank you? I'd like that? You show me yours, I'll show you mine?* Not that an appendix scar was going to compete with a bullet hole, but it was the only scar of any size she had.

She turned onto her side, propping her head in her hand. This was kind of like a sleepover party, only without the other girls, or the pedicures. And there was a strange tension in the air, a current of male/female attraction she was determined to ignore.

"Did you always want to be a cop?"

"Yep. I think so. Too many TV cop shows when I was a kid. Remember *Hill Street Blues?* I used to watch that with my folks when I was a little kid." He laughed, in self-mockery, she thought. "Imagine choosing your career from a TV show."

"I bet it happens a lot. Can you imagine how many kids are planning to be CSI investigators when they grow up?"

"Just pick your city. You're all set." He pulled his arms up, stacked his hands beneath his head, elbows winging out. "How about you? How'd you get into your line of work?"

"An aptitude test."

"Really?"

"Yes. I'm entrepreneurial, enjoy working with people—very important—I'm athletic and interested in anatomy. At one time I thought of being a doctor." She glanced his way, giving a wry grin even though he couldn't see it. "Too much *ER,* probably. But I couldn't face all those years of schooling. Massage therapy suits me better. I'm in partnership with people I respect. And we have a small staff of other wellness professionals. Because we're joint owners, if one of us needs a break it's not a big deal. It's perfect for me."

The rain continued to pound. Sounded like it was settling in for days. Just perfect.

For a few moments they lay there listening.

"Tell me something," he said.

"What?"

"You're smart enough to run your own business, assertive enough to take vacations when you need them, so how come you let your family walk all over you?"

"How can you say that? You've never even met my family." She tried really hard to sound outraged, but it was tough when he was so right. He'd only known her since yesterday and already he'd seen through her to the wimpy soft center she tried to hide.

"I'm a detective, remember? Observing people is what I'm trained to do. The evidence I've collected so far from observing you has been fascinating."

"Fascinating?" Even though he was psychoanalyzing her after a very short acquaintance, it was nice to know he'd bothered.

"Yes. Not entirely in a good way." He pulled his hands out from under his head so he could enumerate on his fingers his evidence. "First, you are planning to wear the butt ugliest dress I've ever seen on a bridesmaid, and believe me, I've seen plenty."

"But I can't help that. The bride always chooses the bridesmaids' dresses. I had no choice but to wear it."

He turned his head and she could tell he was grilling her with his eyes. "Who paid for that orange tent?"

She gulped. "I did."

He nodded and went back to counting off the evidence of her wimpitude. "Second, you spent the first day making some kind of paper flowers."

"Roses. They were roses. A bunch of us got together and made them. It was fun." Although it would have been more fun if the group hadn't been quite so full of older ladies. Most of the young women were working or home with their kids. But it had been nice to catch up with women she didn't see very often.

"Tonight you wrote place cards that could have been hired out or done by someone else."

True, true, true! "I'm the only one in the family who ever learned calligraphy. Plus, I'm reliable. Also, a good speller."

"You let them shove some dentist at you and the only way you can convince them you're not interested is by getting me to front for you as your fake boyfriend."

She was stung. "Well? Isn't that your job, to serve and protect?"

He rolled over to face her. "See? That's what I'm talking about. You're not a wimp with me. You had me damn near terrified last night. If there'd been anywhere to sleep within miles I'd have taken it."

"I know," she admitted, giving up her defensive routine and flopping back on the pillow. "Everything you say is true. I can't seem to help myself. I get around my family and I regress into a doormat. 'Oh, give it to Emily. She won't mind. She's so reliable.'"

"Well? What are you going to do about this little problem of yours? You can't get strange men to pretend to be your boyfriend every time your family pisses you off."

"I don't know." She sighed. "I thought moving away would solve my problem, but it only means higher travel costs to get home for every family occasion. And there are a lot of them."

"Don't you ever say no to them?"

She sighed again. "It's tough being the good girl of your family. It's a lot to live up to. How can I let them down now?"

"I don't know. But if you don't figure it out, you'll spend a lot of your life twisting paper into roses and making small talk with losers you get set up with."

It was humiliating that he could see through her so clearly. She wondered if everyone did.

"What do you suggest?"

"Maybe stop being such a good girl all the time?"

"You want me to be a bad girl? Is that it?" Then realizing how her words could be construed she put her hands over her eyes. "No. Forget I said that."

He chuckled. "If you ever want pointers on being a bad girl, I'm your guy. For instance, do you know that the top female sexual fantasy is having sex with a stranger?"

"How do you know?" she asked, thinking he knew far too much about women.

"I've been around the block. I'm just saying, if that's your fantasy, and you're looking for an easy lesson in crossing to the bad girl side of the street..."

"I'll let you know."

Determined to change a subject that was verging on dangerous given the fact that they were sharing a room and unable to sleep, she said, "Tell me about your family."

"They're great, I'd do anything for them, but I sure as hell wouldn't write a bunch of fancy note cards for their weddings."

She laughed. "Oh, that's not even close to the worst thing I've ever had to do at a wedding."

And that led them to reminisce about all the weddings they'd attended, the good, the bad and the truly ugly.

"Worst wedding ever?" she asked him.

"Easy. Preston and Louise." He had his hands back behind his head and she could see his teeth gleam as he recalled the details.

"Preston and Louise decided to get married on the beach in Mexico. Very romantic, right? So we all flew down to this all-inclusive resort, all on the same flight and everything—the bride and groom, her parents, his parents, the stepparents, the bridesmaids, groomsmen and a few guests and assorted family. There were probably thirty of us altogether. Preston was a buddy from back in high school and he'd always been a heavy partier. I figured he'd grown up. Turns out I was wrong. The all-inclusive part of the resort experience went to Preston's head. All the free drinks and food? He was like a wild man. All but drank Mexico dry of tequila and you never saw him without a plate loaded with food."

"Oh, dear."

"Yeah. Louise wasn't as polite as you. She kept yelling at him every time he was sober enough to understand her, which wasn't that often. So, finally, we have the wedding. It was at sunset, very pretty. We're all dressed up, the minister is great. Louise is so mad at the groom she won't even look at him when she says her vows and when he goes to give her a kiss she turns her head so he gets her cheek."

"You can't blame her."

"No. But it was pretty funny. And he was our buddy, so of course we felt kind of sorry for the guy. Anyhow, we've managed to keep him reasonably sober that day, he's married, we figure our job is done. The wedding reception is a great party, and then Louise wants to go to bed, but nobody can find Preston."

"He'd disappeared on his wedding night?" She could barely believe it.

"Yep. I wasn't the best man that time, luckily, because she lit into poor Mike and then collapsed on his chest, sobbing."

"Mike was the best man?"

"Yeah, sorry. Forgot you don't know them. So we leave Mike with Louise and the rest of us all look for Preston, can't find him anywhere. Mike ends up escorting Louise to the wedding night bungalow, and she's an emotional mess."

"Oh, poor Louise. Did Preston ever turn up?"

"Next morning, a gardener found him curled up under a flowering palm tree. Still in his tux. Passed out cold."

She giggled. "What did Louise do?"

"Had the wedding annulled." He glanced over and his wide grin had her smiling back in anticipation. "Know the best part?"

"What?"

"By the end of the week, Louise and Mike were an item."

"Of course they were. It makes perfect sense that the one she turned to in her hour of need would steal her heart."

"They got married three months later. And because Louise is a waste-not-want-not kind of woman, she reused everything. Same dress, same bridesmaids, same bridesmaid gowns, she even made Preston give her back his wedding ring and she had it resized for Mike."

She laughed aloud at that. "And did she have her second wedding at an all-inclusive?"

"No, ma'am. Louise had learned her lesson. She had the wedding at her parents' home and I doubt there was enough alcohol in the whole house to have got a mouse drunk."

"Poor Louise. I hope she'll end up happy."

"As happy as anyone who believes in fairy tales," he said with a cynicism she found refreshing. "So, your turn. Worst wedding?"

She listened to the rain leaking through the roof taking away her badly needed sleep. Thought about the orange pouf dress that dominated this room she was sharing with a stranger in a bedbug-infested lodge. The setup with Third Cousin Buddy, the pretend boyfriend. "I'm thinking it's going to be this one."

"Well, look on the bright side. At least for this wedding you'll have a great date."

6

"I WOULD NEVER GET MARRIED out of the country," Emily said, ignoring his deliberately provocative comment. And the fact that it was true.

As the buckets filled with water she noticed the tone of the rain hitting the surface changed, growing slightly deeper. She remembered how deep the tubs were and hoped they were big enough that there'd be no overflow.

She was starting to get drowsy in spite of the noise. "What would your wedding be like?" Jonah asked her. "You going for the big fairy tale? Six bridesmaids, arriving at the church in a horse-drawn carriage? That kind of crap?"

She snorted with laughter. "Never, ever in a million years. My ideal wedding involves no tulle, no bridesmaids, no potluck dinners beforehand, no drunk guests trying to look down my top and definitely, absolutely, no 'Ave Maria.' Not sung, not played and not rapped."

"A fifteen minute ceremony at city hall in your jeans?" He sounded vaguely cynical.

"Oh, I'm misting up. You just described my dream."

It was his turn to snort. "Sure I did."

"How about you? What's your dream wedding?"

The silence was the length of ten raindrops in buckets. "I don't plan on getting married."

"You don't believe in marriage?"

"As a matter of fact, I do. It's not perfect, but I think marriage is a fundamental part of a functioning society. It's just not for me. Truth is, I like women too much to imagine tying myself down to one for the rest of my life."

"Maybe you haven't met the right person," she said on a yawn.

"Do you really believe that? Do you think there's only one right person for everyone?"

"I don't know," she said, trying to answer a question she'd thought a lot about over the years. "I don't think I've ever really been in love, so maybe I keep thinking that someday I will and then the whole marriage and family thing will suddenly make sense. Although the older I get the less certain I am." She shrugged, even though he couldn't see the gesture. "I know I want children, so maybe someday I'll realize the big love of my life doesn't exist and I'll settle for a nice guy who'll be there for me and hopefully be a good father to our kids." She sighed. "But I'm not ready to give up on the idea of love yet."

THE SHRILL RINGING OF the telephone woke Emily from a complicated dream concerning bullets, waterfalls and drummers. With a groan, she realized the rain was still pounding down, the shower was going full blast and it was eight-thirty. She and Jonah had talked far into the night. The last time she remembered looking at the clock it had been after four. Apart from wedding stories they'd talked about their jobs, and for a long time about books and movies.

Their tastes weren't identical. He liked more blood-thirsty fiction than she did, and she was more a chick flick kind of girl, but they also had a lot of tastes in common. Especially English mysteries. They'd argued the rival merits of Poirot, Lord Peter Wimsey and Inspector Dalgliesh until she stopped noticing the rain and finally fell asleep. In midsentence as far as she knew for she couldn't remember the conversation ending.

"Hello?" she said into the phone.

"Good morning, darling."

"Morning, Mom."

"Just wondering if you need any help with the place cards?"

Perfect timing. "No. They're all done."

"You're such a marvel. Your aunt and uncle are so grateful for all you've done and you know how proud I am of you."

"That's good. I really don't mind." She thought about her conversation with Jonah last night and how she really did mind, but what was she supposed to say?

"There's something so exciting about a wedding, isn't there? All these last-minute things to do. I'm taking notes, you know. For when it's your turn. See you in a bit."

"Mom, I'm not—" But she was too late. Her mother was gone.

She put the receiver back in the cradle and slowly got out of bed. At that moment the bathroom door opened and emerging in a cloud of steam, like a superhero, was Jonah.

He looked wide-awake and disgustingly cheerful.

"You fell asleep on me last night" were his first words.

"I'm sure you're used to it." She snapped out the

words before thinking. She was mad at herself, her
mother, her aunt, Leanne for choosing that damned
pumpkin of a dress, which was no reason to snarl at
Jonah.

He didn't seem bothered by her snarky remark.
Instead he looked at her as though he wanted to take
her up on her unspoken challenge. "Oh, you think so."
He stalked slowly her way, in nothing but a white towel
wrapped around his waist, stray drops of water spar-
kling in his chest pelt. His hair was slicked back and
clung wetly to his scalp.

The temperature in the room immediately rose and
she wondered what she was thinking, baiting a wolf, if
she didn't want to be bitten. Truth was she'd said the first
flip thing that came to mind, not the smartest thing to
do.

He seemed in no hurry to reach her, so her pulse had
lots of time to speed while he stalked closer. There was
an amused glint in his eyes, and something else. Something she didn't entirely trust that made her want to take
a step back.

She didn't, though. As he came closer, she found
herself searching for the bullet wound he'd told her
about last night. It wasn't that difficult to spot. A jagged
scar that puckered the flesh of his left bicep. She
wanted to raise her hand and trace her finger over the
old wound, an intimacy that shocked her even as the
idea of touching him excited her. It seemed in their
night together of talking they'd sped through the kind
of get-to-know-you conversation that could take weeks
if they'd been dating. Her gaze dropped to the towel
knotted around his hard belly. She imagined him taking
the towel off, looping it around her neck and pulling

her forward. Her gaze shot up to meet his and the way he was looking at her made her wonder if he'd read her mind.

A knock sounded on the door. A reprieve, and she wasn't sure if she wanted to be reprieved.

Jonah veered away from her to answer the door. She could hear a male voice she didn't recognize in the corridor and then Jonah turned to her, still holding the door open, and said, "Okay with you if a sniffer dog comes through?"

"Sniffer dog? You mean there are drugs in this hotel?" What more could go wrong?

He grinned at her. "Bedbug sniffing dogs. The guy says it will only take five minutes."

She threw up her hands. "Why not?" She was still in her pajamas, so she grabbed a hotel robe and threw it on.

A middle-aged man in a uniform sort of like a security guard's brought an energetic beagle trotting in on a leash.

The dog's tail was wagging and his ears were fully alert.

"Okay, Beezer. Go!" the handler said, unhooking the leash, and Beezer was off, sniffing all around both beds. The handler glanced at them oddly and only then did she realize it must seem strange to see two people in a hotel room, one wearing pajamas and the other wearing a towel, who obviously weren't sharing a bed.

She concentrated on watching Beezer. At one point he stuck his nose right between the box spring and mattress, but soon pulled it back out and kept going. He was systematic about his search, she noted, going from bed to bed, then starting on the walls and baseboards.

"How do you know if he finds bedbugs?" She could barely say the word without a shudder.

"Oh, you'll know. He'll wag his tail and bark. Sometimes he paws at the spot."

"How accurate are they?" Jonah wanted to know. Already the dog had moved to sniffing the baseboards in the room. He huffed and snorted his way along. He sounded like a small, powerful vacuum cleaner.

"We claim ninety-eight percent accuracy. But some studies show a hundred percent effectiveness. Dogs like Beezer have an incredible sense of smell."

"Is there enough work to keep you busy?"

The guy grinned at her. "I can't keep up. Ever since DDT got banned, bedbugs are on the rise. It's getting to be a real problem. Nice hotels, dumps, fancy apartment houses, doesn't matter. Bedbugs travel on clothes, suitcases, whatever they can grab on to, and they can live a long time without food. You think of a busy traveler, who might stay at four, five hotels in a week and not realize he's carrying bedbugs until he gets home. Now you've got five hotels with a problem. Plus the guy's got them in his house. Then everyone who stays in every one of those hotels before the problem is caught and fixed? And they go back home or on to another hotel? You do the math."

"You've put me off ever staying in a hotel again," Emily said, feeling her skin crawl.

Beezer stopped at the curtain and looked back at his master, who asked, "What's behind there?"

"A leaky roof."

"You mind?"

"No."

The man in uniform walked over and held the curtain back. Beezer ran in, nose to the floor.

The guy shook his head at her. "With dogs like

Beezer, we can catch problems early and get them fixed right away. My advice is any time you go to a hotel pull back the covers and check the sheets. Same thing before you get into any strange bed."

Beezer trotted out from behind the curtain, zoomed his nose along the remaining baseboards and then the handler opened the closet door. Beezer snuffled his way around, stopping when he got to her bridesmaid dress. He raised his head and looked out at his master, a tent of orange chiffon covering his snout. He returned his attention to the dress as though he was thinking about lifting his leg to it. She couldn't blame him. From his perspective it probably looked like the world's biggest fire hydrant. However, he contained himself, resumed his journey and finished the room. He trotted to the door, his tail wagging, though she thought he looked a little disappointed.

"Good news. Your room's clean."

"What happens if he finds them?"

"He gets a treat. A no bedbug day for Beezer is a bad day."

She laughed, realizing that a good day for room residents was a bad day for the bug sniffing dog. "Can I pat him?"

"Sure, now he's finished working."

She walked over and squatted down, giving the small body a rub. "Good dog, Beezer. Thanks for the peace of mind."

He gave her chin a swift lick, but it was obvious that he wanted to get on with his workday. With a cheery goodbye, the guy in uniform and his dog left them.

"Well," she said when they'd left, "that was different."

"I'd heard about those dogs. Never seen them at work, though."

"Nice to know we're pest free. It's about the only good thing you can say about this room."

"Doesn't sound so bad now. I think the rain's tapered off. I'm heading out in a minute if you want to try to get some more sleep."

"No, it's okay. I've got to go, too, I've got to..." She stopped herself in time. "I've got some shopping to do."

Jonah glanced down at her as though he knew she was heading off on an errand, but he didn't call her on it.

She headed into the shower, which would give him privacy to dress.

"Have a good one," he called a few minutes later.

"You, too."

Before leaving the bathroom, she tidied her cosmetics into her bag. She'd assumed he'd be the messier of the two of them but she'd discovered he kept his few personal items regimented, always in the same corner of the bathroom counter meticulously lined up in the same order. Razor, shaving foam, deodorant, toothpaste (with cap screwed on all the way), toothbrush, floss.

She wasn't a slob by any means, but his neatness quirk intrigued her. She started to leave the bathroom then turned back. What she was about to do was so cliché, so girly she couldn't believe it. Nor could she stop herself. She picked up his razor, dragged it down her cheek, liking the scraping, knowing the same blade had carved through the stubble on Jonah's face. She replaced it exactly, then lifted the lid on his shaving foam and sniffed, recognizing one part of the scent she associated with him. She did the same with his deodorant, then shook her head at herself. What was she doing?

Developing a hot and heavy crush on a guy she barely knew?

What if Beezer and co hadn't knocked on the door when they had?

She recalled the intimacy of that moment when Jonah had walked toward her in nothing but a towel; in retrospect she realized her remark about being used to women falling asleep on him had been a sort of come-on. It had certainly roused him to stalk across the room to her, male ego and testosterone mixing with full throttle desire. Her blood warmed in memory. Jonah might be completely different from her usual taste in men, but there was no denying his animal magnetism. Or that it was drawing her.

If ever there were two people fated to fall in bed with each other, it was her and Jonah. Between the bedbugs, the confused hotel staff and her nosy family, she was sharing a room with a man she didn't know who'd become her boyfriend within twenty-four hours of her setting eyes on him.

Even the weather had conspired, the driving rain keeping them awake and giving them all those intimate hours of the night to talk about everything and nothing the way lovers do.

The only thing they hadn't yet done that lovers do was any of the actual loving.

Maybe, she thought, as she slicked out a piece of Jonah's dental floss to use on her own teeth, maybe she should think about changing that.

She glanced out the window. The rain had slackened to a drizzle but she was probably the only person in Elk Crossing who was hoping for another storm. Because she was almost positive that neither of them could make it through another rain-drumming night without making a move.

She was enjoying her fantasy of making love with Jonah as she rummaged through her few clothes trying to pull off yet another fashion miracle when a soft knock came on the door.

When she opened up she gave a cry of delight. "My clothes!"

She opened her arms to the stuffed dry-cleaning bag hanging from the chambermaid's hand as if it was an old and dearly beloved friend. "I am so happy to see you," she crooned as she took the bag straight to the closet to hang.

The young woman carried a hamper perched on her hip, and Emily recognized her laundered clothes.

"It's not everything," the maid warned her, "but most of your stuff is back."

"This is fantastic." She beamed at the young woman, then went to her purse for her wallet. "Thank you so much."

"I've got more good news," the woman said, accepting the generous tip with a big grin. "We've got a couple of free rooms now. We can move your things today if you want."

Emily's sunny smile faded. "Oh."

She looked at the young woman and suddenly wished she'd never opened the door. What if she didn't know there was a room available? Then she could spend another night with Jonah. Because now that she had a chance to ditch her unwanted roomie, she found she didn't want to. She wanted the night she'd been dreaming about since sometime after midnight when she realized that he was the most exciting man she'd met in a long time.

The maid was looking at her as though trying to figure out what was bothering her. "If it's the bugs, we had the sniffer dog through today. The problem was contained to that one room. The exterminator's been in and of course we won't be renting that one again until we get the all clear. You can trust those dogs, you know. The process is very accurate."

"Only ninety-eight percent accurate," she said primly, thankful for any excuse to put off moving. "I know this room is fine because you never rent it."

"But—"

"Look, I'm kind of in a hurry right now. I'll let you know if I need the room, okay?"

"Sure, but—"

She didn't wait for more; with a friendly smile she closed the door.

Then she looked at the curtain behind which faded plopping sounds could still be heard, and the two rumpled beds. What was she thinking?

7

"I THOUGHT WE WERE GETTING burgers," Sadhu Ranjit said as Jonah headed his truck toward Elk Lodge.

"We are, but I need to grab an extra stick from my hotel first."

They pulled into Elk Lodge's parking lot. "Want to come up?"

"Nah. I'll hang out here and see if I can pick up chicks. I'll woo them with my exotic dark good looks."

Sadhu had more than his fair share of those. He looked like a Bollywood star with his big, brown, thick-lashed eyes and teeth whiter than any shark's. It always amazed Jonah that somebody so pretty was such a formidable ice hockey player. "Just don't do that fake East Indian accent. It embarrasses me." Sadhu had been born in Vancouver and Jonah knew he hadn't been within a thousand miles of the Punjab. But he had the accent down pat and used it shamelessly when it suited him.

Naturally, Sadhu now turned on the voice of his father and uncles as though he'd flipped a switch. "I cannot help it if you do not arrive in time to stop me from meeting beautiful ladies using the voice of my people," he said.

"If you're not here when I come down, I'm leaving,"

Jonah warned, knowing from experience that Sadhu was probably capable of picking up a woman in a hotel parking lot given five minutes. Fortunately, the lot wasn't exactly swarming with attractive women, but Jonah wasn't going to push his luck.

His teammate laughed, flashing his big white teeth. "If I'm not here when you come down, I definitely don't want you coming looking for me."

"Don't forget we've got a game in two hours." Jonah jogged into the hotel and headed for his room. On the way, he all but bumped into a chambermaid with a stack of towels in her arms.

"How's it going?" he asked as he prepared to pass her.

"Great. You're in 318, right?"

He nodded.

"Your clothes came back from the laundry this morning. I put them in your room."

"Good news." Not that he particularly cared except that he'd be glad to see his favorite jeans again. But he suspected his roommate would be weeping with joy at the return of her wardrobe.

"Oh, and the manager told me to tell you both that there are some rooms available now if you want to move into your own space."

He halted in his tracks. Damn it, why had he returned to the hotel? He had a clean shirt and some toiletries in his hockey bag. He wouldn't have been back before bedtime if Mitch hadn't broken a stick this morning in practice.

His metal car keys snicked together as he fiddled with the NHL keychain in his hand. "I see."

It should be great news. His own room—he could

watch whatever he wanted on TV, without the smell of nail polish and other girlie products in his nose; he could come and go without worrying about another person; he wouldn't have to check that he was all covered up when he came out of the shower, or time his stupid shower to fit in with a roommate he'd never asked for or wanted.

But now that he had her he didn't want to get rid of her. Last night had been more fun than he could have imagined a night with an attractive female that didn't include hot sex could be. She was funny, warm, savvy about some things, clueless about others and he had developed some powerful fantasies that involved peeling off those ugly flannel pj's.

"You know, the room's working fine for me. I'm kind of used to the bed now. Don't want to bother moving." He glanced at the girl, realizing that he had no right to keep this information from Emily, who probably would see the situation in a much different light. "I'll let Emily know, though, so she can move."

The woman shook her head over the stack of towels. "Don't bother. I already asked her. She didn't want to move, either."

Jonah couldn't keep the grin from breaking out on his face. "She didn't, huh?"

"Nope." The chambermaid might be young, but she wasn't that young. She regarded him, raising one eyebrow. "Guess you guys are getting on okay after all."

He tossed his keys in the air and caught them with a musical jingle. "Guess so."

He ran into his room—their room—and whistled in time to the percussion coming from behind the curtain.

So, Emily Saunders didn't want to change rooms, huh? That was excellent news.

The room seemed smaller now, with the cupboard crammed full of clothes and Emily's suitcases back from wherever they'd taken them to be fumigated. There was a stack of lingerie sitting on top of the desk, and only the most resolute act of will prevented him from snooping through them. A man could tell a lot by the kind of underwear a woman chose. He liked what he could see from the pile of silk and lace. Suspected he'd like it even more when Emily was in the stuff. Or on her way out of it.

His own clothes were neatly piled on the bed. He picked up his good jeans and, with Emily in mind, skipped his usual T-shirt for a crisply ironed navy blue dress shirt—crisply ironed only because somebody else was wielding the iron. Grabbing his bag, he dug into the side pocket where he'd stashed some condoms, already planning ahead to how and when he'd make his move.

He glanced over at her bed, now so neatly made you could bounce a quarter off the cover. Regardless of the alluring stack of silk on the desk, he hoped she'd wear those flannel pajamas to bed tonight. He'd pictured himself peeling them slowly off her body more times than he wanted to admit. Yep, he'd definitely wait until she was in those flannel things before he made his move.

He dropped the bag with a thunk, his whistle dying as if somebody had strangled it.

Didn't matter, he realized with a sinking sensation in his gut. He wouldn't be making any moves on Emily. Not so long as they were sharing this room.

He'd made her a promise. The words echoed as loudly in the room as the raindrops plopping into the half-filled buckets. He had promised her that so long as they shared this room he wouldn't hit on her.

He must have been out of his mind.

Bending slowly, he replaced the condoms in his bag. Unless Emily found him so irresistible she couldn't keep her hands off him, it looked as though he'd be in for another night of frustration.

Maybe he should simply get himself a new room and save himself the aggravation. But he knew he wouldn't do that.

Jonah was a glass half-full kind of guy. And so long as he and Emily were sharing a room, he could hope.

8

"Not karaoke." Emily groaned the words. But the rest of the girls only giggled.

"It's Elk Crossing on a Thursday night. What else is there to do?" Kirsten Rempel asked.

"See a movie? Give each other manis and pedis? Practice female bonding?"

"It's a stagette night," Ramona argued. "A girl has certain expectations. If she doesn't get drunk, hit on by a male stripper and end with embarrassing photos of herself plastered on Facebook, how will she know her girlfriends love her?"

"Right?" Kirsten added.

"Anyhow, it's ladies' night at Brandy's. The drinks are half-price until eleven."

Of course, Em knew they'd planned the stagette party to coincide with Thursday night at Brandy's. She'd been to enough weddings in Elk Crossing to know every bridal tradition—even the really tacky ones—but she'd sort of hoped now they were all getting older that they might act a little more grown-up. Apparently that wasn't going to happen anytime soon. Not in time for this wedding, anyway.

"At least please tell me we're not dressing up."

An evil chuckle answered her. "Not us, but wait till you see what we've got for Leanne."

THE PATERS CAME OFF THE ICE slowly. The match against the Gettysburg Grandpas had been grueling. Jonah had seriously considered carding the whole team. If these guys were grandpas they were the youngest damn grandparents he'd ever seen. This was an over-thirty league and if those boys had celebrated their big 3-0 it must have been awfully recent.

Contrasted with the youth and vigor of the youngest grandpas in history, his team had seemed old and slow. But, as he'd reminded his team when they groaned their way off the ice between periods, with age comes wisdom. They'd pulled every bit of wisdom and a lot of determination out of their old bones, and sheer strategy had led to a tie game.

Now they were going into sudden death overtime. He tried to ignore the throbbing in his thigh. His roommate had worked some kind of magic with her massage hands, and he was trying to keep up with the exercises she'd given him, but she'd warned him he needed to rest the pulled muscle. He could rest it next week, when he was home.

He sucked back water and wiped the sweat off his face, then before he knew it they were back on the ice.

His opponent won the puck during the face-off. But as he turned to decide where to send it, Jonah scooped it away and flipped the puck to Sadhu who passed it right away down the line to Kevin Lus, their leading scorer.

Kev skated clean and true, hit hard and the puck sailed right by the astonished goalie. They'd won the game in less than two minutes of overtime.

Jonah's leg was throbbing, but he wasn't in the mood to run back to the hotel room and ice the thing again. For one thing, he knew his enticing roomie was out at a stagette party, so he'd be all alone. Somehow the hotel room with the leaking roof wasn't as much fun when he was flying solo.

After a volley of good-natured and mostly rude comments shouted back and forth, the winners and losers decided to hit the town together. They showered and changed to their street clothes. Jonah concentrated on not limping.

"Where should we go?" Sadhu asked.

No one had a clue. The Bar None where they'd spent the previous night was voted down. The draft beer was bad and nobody felt like billiards again.

"Kev should decide. He scored the winning goal."

"Hey, there's the guy who drives the Zamboni. Let's ask him."

Kevin and Sadhu, two of the only single guys on the team, conferred with the Zamboni driver and returned with huge smiles on their faces. "Excellent news, gentlemen. Tonight is ladies' night at Brandy's." Sadhu ran one hand through his thick and lustrous black hair. "You know what that means."

They all groaned. But Sadhu only grinned.

"More action for the Indian Stallion."

"Define *ladies' night*," Mitch said.

Kevin wasn't as much of a looker as Sadhu but he was an enthusiastic partier and rarely went home alone. "Drinks are half-price for the ladies tonight." He rubbed his hands together. "Picture this. A bunch of drunk, horny women. Because there're always male strippers on ladies' night, right? We come in, the new guys from out of town. Fresh meat." He chuckled. "Paradise."

"If there're male strippers, I'm out of there," complained Clark Rasmussen, one of the geezers. "Jonah?"

Since he was team captain, they usually deferred to his opinion.

Ladies' night, huh? In a town this size? Where else would a bunch of girls take a bride for her stagette?

"The strippers will be gone before they let the guys in. Brandy's sounds like a good idea to me."

Kev slapped him on the back and the two teams headed over to Brandy's, which turned out to be a standard cocktail lounge place that had last been updated around 1972. As they paid the six dollar cover charge, Jonah could hear the beat of the music. In fact he could feel it through the soles of his boots. Normally he'd turn tail and run, but he couldn't shake the idea that a bunch of girls having a stagette might end up at ladies' night. In a town this size? Unless they'd organized something in somebody's house, where else were they going to go?

So, he trod down stairs carpeted in purple and red checks and entered a cavernous dimly lit space. Tables were scattered and while the crowd was predominantly female, and a quick glance showed that a bunch of them had taken full advantage of those half-price drinks, the guys were starting to show up.

The hockey players scattered and the married guys found a table in the corner where Jonah knew they'd have a pitcher or two of beer delivered within five minutes. The eager single ones were busy scouting out the action. Jonah preferred to take his time before rushing into anything. He backed up and trod up a couple of stairs until he had a bird's-eye view of the place.

A stage was set up front and center with some speakers and other equipment, but nothing much was happening. A lone DJ type was bent over, fiddling. If male strippers formed part of ladies' night, seemed like they were long gone.

His gaze skimmed the crowd. Some of the women were young and single, obviously on the lookout for some action, and some of the groups appeared to be married women, maybe young moms enjoying a night out away from the responsibilities of home.

And one group was a mixture of young and old, married and not, doing a lot of giggling. In the center of the crowd was an attractive young woman wearing a plastic tiara with a wad of white tulle attached to it, a pink feather boa around her neck, black miniskirt and fishnet stockings. To complete this demure outfit, somebody had attached a ridiculously overstuffed leopard-skin bra to the outside of her clothing. At a wild guess he thought she might be the bride-to-be. Then his gaze moved on and he forgot all about the gal in the tiara.

Emily. There was something about her that caught his attention. Even among a crowd of tipsy, giggling party girls she came across as a class act. When her clothes had come from the local discount store she'd worn them as though Marc Jacobs had personally dressed her in clothing he'd designed with her in mind. But in her own clothes, she was stunning. Her dress was red. Sexy, seductive red that skimmed her body the way his hands longed to. Long, delicious legs ended in high-heeled strappy red sandals.

As he watched her she moved, shifting from where she'd been standing to go talk to the bride. And as she did he realized it wasn't the clothes at all that made her stand out. It was her. The shape of her and the way she moved. Like she and her body liked each other and got along.

He stepped down and started to cross the floor to where she was when a commotion erupted behind him. "There they are!"

And about six seriously inebriated young guys blew past him and headed to where he'd last seen Emily.

He followed at his leisure. Heard a pretend horrified shriek. "This is a stagette, dude! What are you doing here?"

"It's also my stag. There's nowhere else to go in this town on a Thursday night." He watched a drunk young man dragging a plastic ball and chain take the tiara'd young woman in his arms and plant a sloppy wet one on her while copping a feel of her tissue-stuffed bra. "Let's join up."

Jonah was thinking he'd head back to where the married hockey players were sitting, leave Emily be, when one of the stag crowd, older than the rest of the gang, with thinning hair, put a clumsy arm around her. His meaty paw no doubt leaving sweat marks on her red dress.

Jonah was shocked at the visceral punch of annoyance spurting through him. The woman was merely sharing his room in a platonic fashion because of an unfortunate insect situation, and yet he felt as possessive as though they were having amazing sex every night in that room, as if she was his and anybody fool enough to put an arm around her better be prepared to step out in the back alley and swallow his own teeth.

He quickly realized that part of his surge was a protective instinct. Her facial and body language couldn't have been more clear. She didn't want this clown mauling her.

Which was perfect because Jonah didn't want that clown mauling her, either.

He straightened, rubbed his thigh quickly so he wouldn't limp and stepped forward. Emily was pulling away from the beefy guy who was either too drunk or too clueless to realize she didn't want his arm around her. Third Cousin Buddy, he presumed. Well, she'd used him as an excuse on the phone, she was now going to have the opportunity to use him as an excuse to ditch Buddy. In the flesh.

As he approached, he watched Emily tug, with no noticeable effect. She said, "Excuse me," and finally, with an exaggerated sigh, yanked herself free.

"Hey, gorgeous," Jonah said loudly. "Sorry I'm late."

As Emily caught sight of him her face broke out into a huge smile of relief. Anyone watching would think she was in love with him for sure. "Jonah. Am I happy to see you."

She wasn't drunk, not even tipsy, but she'd had a drink or two. Her dark eyes sparkled and her arms came up as naturally as if she greeted him with a hug every time she saw him. It was the simplest thing in the world to pull this sexy woman in red against his chest and accept the invitation offered by her raised face.

He kissed her luscious lips and found them full and soft and tasting faintly of some fruity girl drink. A Cosmopolitan, maybe.

It was supposed to be a little friendly kiss, a signal

to Buddy that she was taken, but then she made a crazy little sound in the back of her throat, a cross between a sigh and a purr, and the scent of her surrounded him and her body fit against his as if they were side-by-side puzzle pieces. Fuzzily, he wondered if maybe she'd had more to drink than he realized and whether he should do the gentlemanly thing and pull away, then her hair swung softly against the skin of his arms, he felt her body press to his and suddenly the little friendly kiss turned deep.

And hot.

And intense.

Everything faded, the noise, the people, the banging beat of the music, and he felt as though there was nothing in the world but the two of them. The kiss deepened, she wound herself tighter against him, his hand reached up to touch her hair, his skin got hotter, her skin got hotter.

"Where have you been hiding *him?*" a loud female voice asked, slurring the words slightly, and suddenly the world came crashing back.

He pulled slowly away, looked into her eyes and saw they were big and amazed. She'd been as stunned by the kiss as he had. "Wow," she whispered.

He could pull away, but he couldn't seem to let her go completely. He kept an arm around her waist, enjoying the feel of her, the long, lean muscles of her back shifting as she breathed.

"What's going on?" demanded the fellow who couldn't keep his meaty paws to himself, the man he was certain was Cousin Buddy.

"Everybody, this is Jonah," Emily managed. She gave an embarrassed giggle. Then she blushed slightly, avoiding his eyes. "My boyfriend."

"Boyfriend?" Buddy stared at him as though it were impossible. "But your aunt and uncle, your parents, all told me you were single."

"I was kind of keeping my relationship quiet." She shrugged and he felt the bunch and stretch all the way down her back. "You know how the family can be."

Jonah might dress in Levi's because that's the brand of jeans he'd always worn and he liked the fit and could not see one single reason why he should advertise some designer's name on his butt and pay hundreds of dollars for the privilege, but he'd also been trained to recognize a lot of brands. It was part of his work as a detective. So, in the few seconds he'd been in the vicinity, he'd cataloged and priced pretty much everything Cousin Buddy was flaunting. The wafer-thin gold watch was more exclusive and a lot pricier than a Rolex. His jeans, artfully faded and distressed, had cost him more hundreds of dollars than anything made out of denim should. His loafers were Italian, probably handmade, and his shirt was from Paris. His eyeglasses, which announced Dolce & Gabbana, weren't knockoffs.

The guy must make a damn good living straightening teeth. Jonah could think of a lot more useful things the man could do with all his money, like fund the overnight shelter for homeless kids in Portland that was near to closing its doors because of funding constraints, instead of plastering his fortune all over his back.

Not that it was Buddy's fault he was a clotheshorse, but it annoyed Jonah on principle to see money wasted on designer clothes that could be put to much better use.

The instant dislike he felt for Cousin Buddy was obviously reciprocated. The pale blue eyes traveled up and down, calculating the value of his wardrobe probably as accurately as Jonah had tabulated his.

Once the dentist had finished his mental tally his nostrils widened in disgust and a contemptuous expression settled over his features. "What exactly do you do, Jonah?" This was said in a "lord of the manor speaking to a peasant" tone that pissed Jonah off. He tightened his arm around Emily. Gave back the same belligerent stare.

"I'm a cop."

The lordly attitude disappeared as though it had never appeared. The pale eyes widened and the dentist's whole body stiffened, mouth pulling down at the edges. "How interesting."

He stuck a fake hearty grin on his face and backed away. "Have a good evening, you two."

And suddenly he was gone.

Now what was that about? Some people had a phobia about police officers, but Buddy had acted more guilty than anything. Jonah suspected a drawerful of unpaid parking tickets.

At least he'd got the guy to back off. Whatever the reason.

Emily rested her head on his shoulder.

"My knight in shining armor," she cooed softly. "Let me buy you a drink."

"I'll get it."

She shook her head. "I owe you. I've been drinking your beer in the room."

"Okay. Thanks." He glanced around; everybody seemed to be drinking mixed drinks, but he'd long ago stopped trying to fit in with the crowd, if he ever had. "I'll have a beer."

He met some of the people she'd told him about, including Ramona, who he remembered was a Wal-Mart employee and struck him as both sharp-featured and sharp-tongued.

Leanne, the bride, gave a whoop and launched herself at him in a hug that left them both winded. "I am so happy to meet you!"

The hug seriously disarranged her fake chest and when she pulled away from him a wad of tissue was hanging out so she looked like a grown-woman-size Kleenex dispenser. She glanced from one to the other. "I knew I was going to like you." And then in a stage whisper they could probably hear back at the ice rink she hissed, "Sweet! Good going, cousin."

Leanne might be at her own stagette party, but she made a point of hanging around to talk with him and Emily. In spite of the ridiculous outfit she was wearing, and the drunken way she'd launched herself at him, he got the sense of a strong protective instinct. She'd be a hell of a mother, and right now he suspected her mothering instincts were on full alert on her cousin's behalf. He liked her right away.

Derek, her husband-to-be, couldn't seem to be in the vicinity without touching his woman. He had a feeling those two would be burning up the sheets tonight.

A pretty blonde with a jagged haircut that looked way too avant-garde for Elk Crossing wandered over. She had a delicate black dress on, bizarre stockings with huge black squares and weird clunky shoe-boots that he imagined were pretty stylin'. He counted eight earrings in one ear, and couldn't help but wonder how much it had hurt to drill the silver post through the cartilage where her ear met her face. Beneath her sexy demeanor was a wistfulness he found intriguing.

She sank to a seat across from Emily. Her eyes searched the surrounding area like a child looking for a lost pet.

"Jonah, this is Kirsten."

They shook hands and he noticed that her black nail polish was a mess. Like she'd gnawed most of it off. She sat there for a minute. "What time is it?" she asked Emily.

"Around ten, I think."

Once more the pretty brown eyes searched the area.

"Did you lose something?"

She took a sip of her drink, looked down into a black leather bag, pulled out a pack of cigarettes and then shoved it back again. "My boyfriend was supposed to meet me here."

"Are you still seeing Tyler?" Emily asked.

She glanced down before nodding her head. As though she was ashamed.

"How's the job hunt going?"

Kirsten shrugged. "There's not much in my field."

"Not in Elk Crossing. There's not much in anyone's field in Elk Crossing. Are you looking in bigger cities?"

"Of course I am. I want something better. But it's not that easy to find a job in promotions, not in this economy."

"I know. But you're smart and bright and have all kinds of potential. It'll happen."

Kirsten looked down at her hands and began to scratch the polish off one nail with another. Which he supposed was slightly less unsightly than gnawing it off. "Tyler wants us to move in together, so we can save some money."

There was a beat of silence. He didn't know Emily all that well but he could sense from the way her body tightened beside him that she thought this was a terrible idea.

"Doesn't Tyler still live with his mother?"

"Yeah. We'd both live there. She's fixing up her basement for us. But I don't really want—"

"Jonah, so that's where you've been hiding yourself," a grinning Sadhu said loudly, approaching the three of them. His teeth were so white you'd have thought he'd stopped to polish them on his way to the table.

Next to Emily, Kirsten was the hottest woman in the room. He was surprised it had taken his buddy so long to get here.

"My teammate Sadhu," he said. "And this is—"

"Hey, guys," a new male voice said behind him.

He bowed to the inevitable, not even surprised that the two single Paters were suddenly his closest friends. It was now official. Leanne's stagette included the hottest women in the bar. "And this is Kevin."

The players introduced themselves and as Kevin stepped forward to Kirsten, Sadhu cut him off as smoothly as he'd cut off the Gettysburg Grandpas on their way to the net, stealing the puck with so much stealth they barely noticed it was missing until he'd scored.

"I didn't catch your name clearly," Sadhu said, slipping into the vacant seat beside her. "Was it Kirsten or Kristen?"

Kevin didn't waste a lot of time on a lost cause. He

took a swift glance around and settled on a well-endowed redhead named Lisa.

Tyler, his mother and her basement seemed forgotten as Kirsten let herself enjoy Sadhu's attentions. He was good at making a woman feel as if she was the only woman in the room, in the whole world, and soon Kirsten had stopped peeling away her nail polish. When she laughed, she even lost her wistful expression.

Kevin and Lisa were getting on almost as well. Leanne and Derek were dancing so closely he hoped they'd remembered birth control.

Jonah was surrounded by couples who were on their way to getting lucky.

Unlike him. He took a sip of beer.

He'd made Emily a promise that he wouldn't hit on her and he tried to be a man of his word, but never had he regretted a promise more.

He had a feeling, once they got back to the room and went to their separate beds, it was going to be a long, uncomfortable night.

If only he hadn't kissed her.

9

"AND NOW, LADIES AND GENTLEMEN," the DJ boomed into his mic, "ladies' night at Brandy's continues with our famous Thursday Night Karaoke."

"Karaoke? You're kidding me." Jonah glanced at the people around him with an expression of acute horror. Sadhu and Kirsten were too busy to notice. But Emily answered him.

"I wish it was a joke. Welcome to the biggest excitement in Elk Crossing on a Thursday night."

Jonah had shaved again since this morning, she was certain, but even so she could see the faint beard under his skin. He smelled good and the navy cotton shirt covered a torso she'd been eyeing for days.

Why had she kissed him? All she could think about was how great his mouth had felt against hers, how her body had leaped to life and she'd all but crawled into his clothes when their bodies had touched.

The only good thing was that the kiss had made Buddy back off, but she knew she was playing with fire. As far back as nursery school when she'd read all those fairy tales, she'd learned that it was never a good idea to tease a wolf.

Especially if you happened to be sharing a hotel room with him.

The DJ started things off with a rousing rendition of "Lady."

After the applause died down he yelled out, "I hear we have a hen party tonight. I want to call on Leanne the bride to come up and give us a number."

"No," Leanne shrieked. "No."

But her friends Ramona and Lisa dragged her up to the stage with loud encouragement from the audience. Once at the mic, she held on to the pair of them so tightly that they ended up singing "Like a Virgin" as a trio. Very badly. And with a lot of giggling. The shout-outs coming from the stag party and Sadhu and Kevin weren't helping.

"I need to get out of here," Jonah said after they'd finished. "My ears can't take this kind of pain."

He chose an unfortunate moment to rise, for the DJ immediately stuck a spotlight on him. "All right. Our next contestant."

"No," he said, but Leanne was grabbing him by the hand; obviously happy now that her ordeal was over to force other innocents into karaoke hell. The wedding party were all cheering, and Emily took one look at his face and started laughing so hard she had tears in her eyes.

When Leanne used her free hand to grab on to Emily and tug her to her feet, suddenly it wasn't so funny.

"No, Leanne. We don't want to sing. We were leaving."

"It's my party and you'll sing if I want you to." Then she giggled. "That's almost a song."

"Okay, folks," said the DJ after they'd been dragged up to the stage. "What are you going to sing for us?"

"Give them a love song duet. They're so in love," Leanne called out, her voice beginning to sound hoarse.

He took one look at the pair of them and said, "I've got exactly the song right here. Come on up, folks. Here's a microphone for you, ma'am. And one for you, sir."

Emily blinked through a spotlight to look out at the crowd, her own people hooting and cheering, and then at Jonah, who seemed to be as stunned as she.

The DJ fiddled with his machine, and said, "I've chosen something very special for you two lovers.

"Now, follow the bouncing ball and sing along with the words." The DJ clapped them both on the shoulder. "Have fun."

She glanced down at the screen and groaned. "No."

But the music had already started. She looked up and Jonah was giving her that laughing look that for some reason reminded her of the steamy kiss. It seemed to her that in that moment they made an unspoken agreement to get through this thing with as much style as possible. Retreat was out of the question and butchering the song seemed a little cruel to the people stuck listening to them. Besides, Emily could sing.

The DJ said, "Let's hear it for Emily and Jonah singing Sonny and Cher's 'I Got You Babe.'" Amid laughter, clapping and cheers, their cue arrived. She leaned closer to her mike. Jonah did the same, holding her gaze.

They sang.

He had a pretty good voice, too, she discovered, and seemed to feel that now they were up here, they should give the crowd something that was at least in tune.

Emily had performed in all the high school musicals, so she soon fell into performance mode, rusty though it might be.

The secret, she recalled her drama teacher telling them, to handling something really cornball was to play it straight. So she acted like she was Cher singing to her Sonny, and they were in love, except that he was Jonah and it wasn't love she was feeling but a serious case of lust. When she belted out the lyrics, she pictured the two of them in that hotel room all night long and something in her tone must have expressed her sudden desire, or maybe it was the bump and grind she did with her hips, because the air grew thick with wolf whistles.

When the song ended, Jonah pulled her to him for a kiss, and the crowd went wild. Well, Leanne and Derek's wedding party went wild and they were loud enough for everyone.

It was only supposed to be a silly kiss, she was certain, to accompany a karaoke duet of equal foolishness, but the second their mouths fused she felt the heat between them, the power of their mutual attraction, and everything inside her began to hum.

Naturally, the wolf whistles, hoots and hollers only grew louder. Laughing, a little embarrassed and a lot turned on, she pulled away, executed a curtsy that would have impressed the queen of England and ran off the stage. Jonah was right behind her.

She got back to their table and noticed he was no longer with her.

"Oh, my God," shrieked Leanne, "I'd forgotten you could sing."

"Really, I can't. I was only goofing around."

The bride leaned closer. "You and Jonah are so hot together. Phew." She fanned herself, sending the tiara with a pouf of tulle attached sliding down over one ear. "No wonder you're always in such a hurry to get back to your hotel."

Instinctively, Emily's gaze turned to where her internal radar informed her that Jonah was. He was leaning against one of the tables, a bottle of beer halfway to his lips, and he was looking at her. *S-i-z-z-l-e.*

His eyes looked so dark from here she could lose herself in their shadow. His posture was casual but she felt that every cell of his body was alert. Waiting for her. For them.

And how every cell in her body responded. Her heart sped up, her breathing grew suddenly shallow, and her skin started to tingle.

He lifted the bottle to her in a silent toast.

"You're leaving, aren't you?" Leanne demanded. Then she looked over at Jonah significantly. "Not that I blame you. He is hot."

She followed her cousin's gaze. "I know." However, she was at a stagette and took pride in not being the kind of woman who dumps her girlfriends when her guy shows up, so she said, "He'll still be hot when I get him home. I'm in no hurry." *Liar.*

"Good. Have another drink. It's my bachelorette party and I insist." The tipsy bride waved down their cocktail waitress.

"Drinks for my bridesmaids."

Emily sent a helpless look to Jonah. She wanted to leave. With him. Now. But she was also well aware that her duties as a bridesmaid included seeing Leanne through to the end of the night. She was sort of hoping that Derek could speed up the end of the stagette, but he was off laughing and joking with his friends so it didn't seem as though that was going to happen.

As she settled back onto a bar stool, her cell phone rang. How annoying was that? "Sorry," she said to

Leanne, who hadn't even noticed with all the other commotion going on around them. She picked up the phone and flipped it open, before she realized that it wasn't a call, but a text message. Her partners often texted her about things, so she pressed the icon.

The message read:

Pickup confirmed. Saturday. Midnight.

Huh?

"What are you doing with my phone?" Buddy stormed toward her from the direction of the men's bathroom looking irate.

Instinctively she pulled the phone back from his outstretched palm. "It's my phone."

But even as she pulled the phone her way the obvious truth hit her. This wasn't her phone. It didn't have the right heft in her palm. Its shape was slightly different.

She looked down at the phone. "Sorry," she said sheepishly. "I thought it was mine. Here."

Instead of being nice about an honest mistake he grabbed the cell from her, his eyes narrowing in fury. "Did you answer it?"

"No."

She'd read a text, which wasn't the same thing as answering a phone, and based on the way he was already glaring at her she certainly wasn't going to tell him what she'd done.

It had been an innocent mixup.

Fortunately, at that moment a welcome diversion occurred. The DJ was booming over the sound system once again. "Here's a special song dedicated to our bride, Leanne."

They all looked around and Leanne cried out, "Derek, what are you doing?" She glanced at Emily in mock panic. "He can't sing. And he's shy. What is he doing? He must be drunk."

But Derek didn't seem particularly drunk, not that they were perhaps in the best state to judge. He found Leanne in the crowd and said, "I want to climb a mountain for you, slay a dragon with my bare hands, write your name in the clouds to prove how much I love you. But I guess you know how hard this is for me." He gulped and they could see his Adam's apple bob. "I love you, Leanne."

"Oh, Derek," Leanne said, grabbing a tissue from her overstuffed bra and wiping her eyes. "I love you, too."

Derek wasn't the greatest singer in the world and Emily wasn't sure the king himself would have recognized this version of "Love Me Tender," but she didn't remember when she'd felt so emotional over a sentimental old love song.

The way Derek was looking at Leanne, as though his heart and soul belonged to her, was enough to touch even a confirmed cynic and Emily found herself reaching into the leopard bra cups for her own tissue. Between herself, Leanne and the rest of the stagette girls, Leanne went from a double D to a B cup before the song was over.

Nobody was ever going to mistake Derek for Harry Connick Jr. but neither could anyone doubt the depth of his love for his bride. The audience was surprisingly silent as he sang his way through the verses, but responded with rousing cheers and applause when he was done.

Leanne just got out of her seat and ran toward him, launching herself into his arms as he descended from the stage. She jumped up, wrapping her legs around his waist and her arms around his neck. "I love you," she sobbed.

Derek just hoisted her higher, gave a single-handed wave to the two stag groups and kept walking in the direction of the exit.

"Well," Ramona said after the bride and groom had left and a stunned silence ensued. "I think the stagette is officially over."

10

EXCITEMENT, ANTICIPATION, a thrill of nerves skittered through Emily's system as she opened the door to the hotel room she and Jonah were sharing. He was right behind her and she could swear she could feel his body heat as he stood there.

She'd probably been this sexually primed, pumped up, excited, horny before. She simply couldn't remember when. But then she'd never in her life experienced foreplay in the form of a leaky roof or karaoke, either.

Jonah had been uncommonly silent on the ride home, which she assumed was his way of coping with an attraction she knew he felt as strongly as she.

The door opened. She stepped inside, almost smiling when she heard the steady drip of the leaking roof spilling into the buckets. Her body stirred.

She stepped away from the door, watched Jonah enter and take his time locking up behind him. She'd pictured them throwing themselves at each other the second the door shut, but she was a little hesitant. All she needed was the slightest move from him and she'd be in his arms.

He paused. Looked at her. A second ticked by. Three. Five. He scowled. "You want to use the bathroom first?"

Was he fussy about kissing a woman before she'd brushed and flossed? She had no idea, but some of her lust was cooling. He seemed so strange. Grumpy, almost.

"Okay. Sure."

She put down her purse, toed off her heels and headed for the bathroom. The stack of her good lingerie was on the desk waiting to be put away. She'd assumed she'd be naked by now, instead she was trying to decide whether she should slip into one of her sexy nighties or what. It didn't help that Jonah was watching her every move like a guy looking for trouble.

"Don't forget your pajamas," he said curtly. "The maid put them under your pillow."

Your pillow? Weren't they going to be sharing? The way they'd been kissing earlier tonight she'd been so sure.

What was he doing? Some kind of teasing game? Screw him. "I'm going to take a shower," she said as she grabbed the ugly flannel and stalked into the bathroom. She showered, scrubbed her face free of makeup and brushed and flossed thoroughly. When she emerged, she found Jonah with a pillow at his back, his eyes glued to a nature show on television, though she had a sense he wasn't taking any of it in.

"Your turn."

He glanced up and his scowl deepened.

What?

She got into bed, not knowing what else to do, and pretended to read a magazine. She flipped a few pages. She wasn't interested in this season's fashions right now. *Flip.*

A recipe for low-fat guacamole. Yeah, that's what was missing in her life. *Flip.*

Eyeliner tips. She didn't wear the stuff. *Flip. Flip. Flip.*

The pages snapped as she turned them. "Six Secrets to Help You Scorch the Sheets Tonight." Hah! Not the way this night was going. She tossed the magazine toward the trash but her aim was off and it hit the desk and flopped to the floor, pages fanning out messily.

Jonah, naturally, chose that moment to come out of the bathroom wearing his athletic shorts and a black T-shirt. More than he usually wore to bed.

He paused, looking down at the magazine spread out at his feet.

"'Scorch the sheets Tonight'? Who comes up with this crap?" He bent down, picked up the mangled magazine and, putting it back together, placed it on the desk.

Then he stopped. Glared at her one more time. Even longer than when he'd done it when they'd first entered the room. Then with a mumble she couldn't quite catch but that sounded vaguely like a curse, he stomped to his bed, threw back the covers as though they had personally insulted him and needed to be punished, and shoved himself into his own bed.

He lay rigid on his back staring at the ceiling. All the casual intimacy of earlier tonight was gone. He was like a different man. A storm cloud with five o'clock shadow.

"What is your problem?" she finally asked.

"I'm a damned fool."

She rolled her eyes. "I know that. Why should that put you in such a bad mood all of a sudden?"

"Because you women are all the same."

"What?" It was such a blatantly odd and untrue

statement and he seemed so put out that some of her irritation was replaced by simple curiosity.

He snapped off the nature show, rather the same way she'd flipped pages on her magazine. It occurred to her that he was as sexually frustrated as she was.

He turned to glare at her. "You want equality, the same pay as men, share the housework and childrearing and God forgive the poor fool who tries to open a door for a woman or pull out her chair."

"I like having the door held for me," she said, wondering what he was talking about.

His answer was a bitter snort. "And when it comes to the bedroom? You all act like it's the nineteen-fifties. I don't see you sharing the workload there. Where's the equality in that?"

"I'm not following you. If you're referring to me, how do you know what I'm like in bed? We don't seem to be going there."

"Whose fault is that?" he bellowed in outrage. "I told you, in this very room, that I wouldn't make a pass at you. I promised you. And I try to be a man of my word. So we come back to the room, after a night when you threw plenty of encouragement my way, I might add—" here he stabbed a finger in her direction "—but do you follow through on what you started? No."

"But—"

"Do you seduce me? No." He crossed his arms over his chest and shoved his back once more against the pillow behind him on the wall. "Well, I'll be damned if I'm going to spend another night in this room having erotic fantasies about those flannel pajamas of yours."

He got out of bed and started for his jeans. "I'll go to the front desk and see about another room."

A gurgle of laughter escaped her. She glanced down at her nightwear. "Are you kidding me? You were having erotic fantasies about these?"

"I'd appreciate you not laughing at my sex fantasies. They're my business."

She felt suddenly a million times better. This night wasn't going to be a disaster at all. All she had to do was make the first move.

He'd paused with his jeans in his hands. Wasn't exactly making any effort to insert his legs into them.

"So, what you're saying is that in order to have sex with you I'm going to have to seduce you?"

His gaze when he turned her way was smoldering. And slightly less grumpy. "Yeah. Not so much fun when the boot's on the other foot, is it? When you're the one who has to do all the work."

"Right. I can see that it's tough being a guy trying to get a woman into bed." She shook her head at him. "Then you have to face the possibility of rejection."

He looked as though he wanted to argue with her about the rejection thing, but he didn't. He merely said, "Exactly."

"And all that performance anxiety," she added with false sympathy. "It's tough out there."

His gaze squinted like a tough guy in a shoot-out. "I never said I suffer performance anxiety."

"I'm glad to hear it."

He glanced over, a calculating expression in his eyes. "But we still have the basic problem."

"And that is?"

"If you want sex tonight, lady, you're going to have to do something about it."

She sighed. Pulled the covers all the way back so he could get his fill of the flannel pj's he apparently liked so much.

"But that's a problem."

"What is?"

"I'd like to have sex with you." She swallowed, since merely saying the words gave her a secret thrill. "But the truth is, you're right." She leaned back on her arms, knowing the move pressed her breasts tight against the buttons of the pajamas. "I'm usually the one who gets seduced."

She could feel his gaze on her, feel his attention on her breasts which was making her as hot as though his hands were on her.

"Uh-huh."

She shifted, letting the fabric ride up so a length of skin appeared between the waistband of her bottoms and the edge of the top. "What I'm probably going to need is a little help."

He watched the edge of skin appear. "You're killing me. You know that, don't you?"

His voice was low, the passion contained about as well as an overfilled dam that was getting ready to burst.

She ignored his comment.

"Do you think you could do that?"

"Do what?"

She glanced at him from under her lashes. "I'm thirty-one years old and I've never ever seduced a man. I wouldn't know the first thing to do."

"Sure you would."

"Wait. Pass me that magazine. I should read that article."

"You don't need any magazine article and we both know it."

It was difficult not to give in to the smile that kept trying to pop out on her mouth. God, he was cute. "Then maybe you could give me a lesson in how to seduce you?"

11

"OH, HONEY, I'LL GIVE YOU a lesson in how to seduce me all right. It's easy. Get your sweet ass out of that bed, take off those pajamas and put yourself in this bed with me."

Jonah couldn't believe how well this night was turning out after it had seemed doomed. But what he hadn't counted on was that when he explained his problem, Emily would turn it into a sexual game. One he wasn't sure he could survive.

He wanted that woman so much it hurt. Especially now she was forcing him to wait. Teasing him with her fake helpless routine when she knew exactly what she was doing.

She wrinkled her nose at him now, not even bothering to conceal the laughter in her eyes. "Take off my clothes and get into bed with you? That's it? That's your idea of seduction?"

He nodded strongly.

"Isn't that kind of…fast?"

He nodded again, just as hard. "See, that's the thing about men. We're real simple when it comes to getting us into bed. Most of the time all you have to do is show up."

She shifted to face him, extending her legs so her

feet rested on the edge of his bed. The pants of those ugly pj's of hers rose above her ankles and he was consumed by a desire to kiss the bumps of bone. Her toes were painted a sassy red and as he regarded the little bit of naked skin she'd allowed into his bed he found himself halfway to a foot fetish.

"I think, if you don't mind, for my first effort I'd like to move on to something a little more advanced."

Advanced, ha. This woman had been seducing men since she first figured out the difference between boys and girls.

She was one of those women it came as naturally to as breathing. He doubted she was even conscious of her power.

He wanted to wrap his hand around her ankle, he could all but feel the shape of her, the silky warmth of her skin. He wanted to trace the shape of her legs slowly up to her thighs. First on the outside of the flannel covering her legs, and then he'd peel them slowly down her legs.

But he wasn't going to do that. Not yet. As much as it was killing him to wait, this was her game and she was playing it for all she was worth.

"Advanced techniques?" He shook his head. "Are you sure you're ready? You seem like a rank amateur to me. Maybe you'd be best to take my advice and start nice and easy. Trust me. Get naked. It'll work."

Once more she shifted, letting her legs ease apart, leaning on one hip so the buttons of her top strained and he could see the outline of her breasts, a glimpse of cream-colored skin in the gape of the fabric.

"I'm not sure about this. I won't even know what to do with my hands." She held them up for him and the visceral punch of lust suckered him as he imagined those capable massage therapist's hands on the hottest part of his body.

"Get over here and I'll show you," he said, barely keeping his tone even.

She licked her lips, slowly, as if they were covered in honey. "Why don't you tell me what you want?"

"Take off your top."

She looked at him slantwise from under her lashes, her eyes gleaming at him. She raised her hands languidly to the first button. He watched her ease the plastic disk out of the buttonhole, taking a long, long time about it. Every part of him strained to reach across and help her speed up the operation, but they both knew he wouldn't, which only added to the torture.

Her fingers moved to the second button. Paused.

"I don't know," she said, "I feel strange taking off my top while yours is still on."

"This is your show," he reminded her, settling back and deciding to enjoy this strangest of seductions.

"Maybe you could take your shirt off," she whispered.

"Okay."

He reached for the hem. Prepared to yank the cotton over his head.

"But not too fast. We had male strippers at Brandy's earlier tonight. It was fun watching them. Not that I want you to think I expect you to be of that high caliber or anything."

He snorted. "That's a relief."

"I want to watch you peel your shirt off nice and slow." Her voice seduced him, the idea of her watching him strip excited him. He slid the cotton slowly up his belly, feeling incredibly foolish until he noticed her gaze fastened on to his emerging belly.

"I feel like you might stuff some money in my G-string if you like what you see."

She grinned at him. "I might at that."

He pulled the shirt all the way over his head, going as slowly as he could, knowing she was having fun, enjoying himself more than he'd have thought possible while waiting so long for some action.

Once he was naked from the waist up, he looked pointedly at her. "Now you."

She unbuttoned the second button. The third. She'd stopped tormenting him, as though realizing he was close to the end of his rope. Maybe she was feeling the same way.

The air felt increasingly hot around them; the slower paced plops of water behind the curtain added a drumbeat to the slow striptease.

He'd fantasized about slipping that flannel off her body, but never imagined her doing the job. He liked to watch her doing the peeling just fine.

"How am I doing?" she asked as she got to the last button.

"Perfect."

She slipped the last button through the hole. Held the two sides of the fabric together.

"Do you think you could get that top off before the wedding on Saturday?"

"In a hurry, aren't you?"

"You have no idea."

And just like that, the game ended. She slipped the pajama jacket off her shoulders, let it slide down her arms in a dowdy heap, leaving her exposed in all her beauty.

"You're even prettier than I imagined," he told her honestly, leaning forward to cup her breasts in his hands.

"Mmm," she murmured, pushing forward into his palms, encouraging him to explore, to play.

He took full advantage of her offer, kneading, tweaking, running his hands down her belly, which was taut with muscle, lean like a runner's.

Her eyes were big and glistening with passion.

"Your bed or mine?"

"Both," he promised her, and leaning forward decided it was well past time that he joined in on this seduction. He took her mouth, took it in the way he'd dreamed of since he first tasted her earlier in the evening.

He took his time, exploring her mouth, teasing her lips, making her sigh. He let his mouth go all the places it wanted to go. Her shoulders, her upper chest, which he discovered was incredibly sensitive, then the swell of her breasts. Her nipples, which looked like tiny raspberries and tasted like heaven.

When he nuzzled her belly she giggled and squirmed. "You should have shaved."

"I did," he told her. "And that was an act of pure, desperate hope."

He felt the quiver of her skin beneath his lips. "I couldn't believe you didn't jump me the second we got into the room."

"You have no idea how much I wanted to," he murmured into her belly button. "How much I still do."

He hooked his thumbs into the elastic waistband and she obligingly lifted her hips so he could slide the fabric down, down, down.

Her skin was so soft, the springy curls between her legs were soft, he kissed his way down as he drew the pajama pants down and off.

She lay there, looking up at him expectantly. Knowing neither of them could take much more teasing, he yanked off his shorts, kicking them to the side so they landed in a heap atop her discarded pajamas.

He found the condoms he'd dropped back into his bag and placed one at the ready.

The rain increased in intensity and the drumbeat behind the curtain rose in tempo. He grinned down at her. "I have to tell you that every time I hear a raindrop from now on I am going to get horny."

"Quit talking and get down here."

"Yes, ma'am."

He rolled into her bed beside her and took her in his arms, letting their bodies touch and meld, skin to skin, heart to heart, mouth to mouth.

She started to move, undulating against him, exciting them both. He let his hands explore, teasing her until she was panting, then finding her wet center and preparing her.

Those massage therapist's hands knew exactly how and where to touch him for maximum effect. Light touches, stronger touches, until he was panting, as well.

It was she who put the condom on him, then eased herself onto him, taking over the seduction once more. When he entered her body it was as if he was trying something completely new.

Her eyes were shut, her body clamping him already as she started to ride him. He wondered if he even realized she was following the beat of the raindrops.

He reached for her breasts, grabbed her hips, followed the rhythm she set until she gasped, clutching his shoulders, leaning forward to kiss him as her climax took her.

What could he do but follow?

12

KARAOKE WAS OVER, MOST OF HER friends had gone home and Kirsten was still here. She was a little drunk and very cranky. Tyler hadn't shown up, after he'd promised her. Not that she should be surprised. Tyler's promises were more in the "if I feel like it and get around to it" category than actual commitments.

She wished he'd shown up if only so he could see another guy hitting on her. A gorgeous one at that. But now the evening was coming to an end and on top of being stood up by her boyfriend she was now going to have to blow off Sadhu who was clearly hoping she was going to take him home with her.

Ramona came by to say goodbye, looking pointedly at Sadhu, her mind already in gossip mode.

"Do you have a ride home?"

Both to stop her from gossiping and to let Sadhu know what was up, she said, "Yeah. Tyler's coming for me." Even though she doubted he even remembered he'd promised.

"Okay." Ramona smiled her fake smile and said, "I never got a chance to meet you. I'm Ramona."

"Sadhu." He shook her hand.

"You from around these parts?"

God, she was nosy. Kirsten had no idea why Leanne

and the rest of them insisted on being friends with such an annoying person. As if her night wasn't weird enough, she now had Ramona to deal with at two in the morning.

"My family is from the Punjab, where the cow is sacred and every man is master in his own home." A strange choking sound came out of her throat as she heard an East Indian accent come out of Sadhu that he must have copied from *The Simpsons*. Of course, Ramona had no idea she was being made a fool of. Suddenly, Kirsten wasn't quite so tired.

"Well, it's different over here, of course," Ramona told him seriously. "We like to eat cows. And my husband sure isn't the master of me." She tittered. "But I love Indian food."

"Where I come from, we call it food," he replied in that same accent.

It took her a minute to get the joke, then she laughed and wished him a good trip.

"That is a really bad accent," Kirsten told him once they were alone.

"Not at all, I assure you." He dropped back to his usual voice. "Anyhow, she pissed me off. I don't like being patronized, especially not by somebody who's never been outside of Idaho. Somebody fed her curried chicken one time and now she's an expert on Indian food."

She laughed. "Okay. I officially like you."

He grinned at her. He was good-looking and knew it. Usually she hated those kind of guys, but somehow with Sadhu she felt like he didn't take it all that seriously.

"Who's Tyler?" he asked. A logical question. With no logical answer.

They'd been talking for hours, and she thought she'd probably told him most of her life story. But somehow Tyler hadn't come up in conversation.

"He's sort of my boyfriend."

Sadhu looked around at the nearly empty room. They'd already had last call and people were leaving. Nobody new was coming in. "He's not picking you up, is he?"

"Probably not."

"He got a good excuse?"

She sighed. "Probably not."

He rose. "Come on. I'll drive you home."

She took the hand he held out to her and got to her feet, stumbling slightly. If there was anybody sober enough to drive her, it was him. He'd been on soda water all night. "How come you don't drink alcohol?"

He opened his mouth and she stopped him. "And don't give me any crap about 'your people.' You're as American as I am."

"Okay. The truth is, my mother really hates it and I never got the big thrill out of getting drunk. I'd rather have a clear head when I'm playing sports." He glanced at her through the thickest, silkiest eyelashes she'd ever seen on a man. "And especially when I'm spending time with a beautiful woman."

"Huh." She wished she were a little clearer-headed right now.

As they walked out, he took her hand in a loose grip that felt friendly and yet warm and a little sizzling as their palms touched. Unlike his ridiculously girlish eyelashes, his hands were tough man hands. Callused from all those sports, she supposed, but the fingers that threaded hers were long and supple. She imagined them touching her body and felt an insane surge of desire.

He led her to a green SUV, and when she got inside she noticed it was spotless. He climbed in and started the engine.

He turned to her, dark and mysterious in the dim light. "Where to?"

She reviewed her options. She instinctively shrunk from taking him to her place. Not only was it a mess, but who knew when Tyler would remember she existed and maybe drop by.

"Your place?" she suggested.

"Too crowded. I'm sharing a hotel room with two other guys." He tapped the steering wheel. "Your place?"

"Too complicated."

"Want me to just drop you off?"

"No." She knew he was a player who only wanted to get her into bed, but it was so nice to have this kind of attention. And he made her feel good about things. No, she wasn't ready for the night to end.

"Well, this is your town. Where do two people go in the middle of the night?"

She grinned at him, feeling like a kid again. "There are basically two options. You can go to the all-night diner just out of town, or you can go parking by the lake." She felt about sixteen again. "Want to go parking?"

His teeth gleamed in response. "Sure."

She directed him down a series of roads to one that ended in gravel and overlooked the lake. A few fishing cabins with docks awaited summer, but if anyone was staying out here on a Thursday night in November, they were already in bed. The place felt dark and deserted. The lake was a huge expanse of darkness, stippled with raindrops, tiny waves lapping the sodden shore.

She felt a sudden burning need for a cigarette. She reached for her smokes and the door handle simultaneously. "I'm guessing you don't like people smoking in your car. I'll go outside."

"I didn't know you smoked." He sounded disappointed. Probably one of those guys who were disgusted by cigarette breath. Great. "You didn't smoke all night."

She slumped back against the seat. "I'm trying to quit."

"Maybe you should try harder."

"What's that supposed to mean?"

"It means either be a smoker or a nonsmoker. Anything in between sounds too undecided."

She looked at him, trying to figure out where the man who'd been so hot for her all evening had suddenly disappeared to.

"You know, you're a really interesting person. Beautiful, bright, sexy. Why would you put up with a guy who doesn't remember to come and get you? The guy sounds like an asshole."

"It's not like there are a lot of guys to choose from in Elk Crossing."

Which was why she was here, she supposed. Well, if there was one thing she knew how to do, it was to get a guy interested in her.

Leaning over, she ran her fingers up his arm, scooched over so they were in easy mouth-reaching distance of each other, dropped her voice to a murmur. "Maybe you should take my mind off cigarettes."

She'd give him a second to make a move on her and if he didn't she'd move in on him.

But he didn't move on her. To her shock she heard the engine start up. Her eyelids flew open. "Put your seat belt on and give me directions to that diner. I swear to God I've never said this to a woman in my life, but we have to talk."

They said barely another word until they were in Earl's Diner. She ordered coffee, because it was three in the morning and she didn't know what else to have. He ordered coffee, too, but told the waitress to leave the menu.

Earl's was the kind of diner you still find outside small towns. Family-owned, it catered to the truck trade, shift workers and kids who stayed out too late. Other than a heavyset guy in a baseball cap eating a chicken pot pie and drinking soda, yesterday's newspaper spread in front of him, they were the only customers.

She was prepared for anything including an admission that Sadhu was gay or a grilling about her sexual health, but she was still shocked when, after dumping too much milk and sugar into his coffee he sat back and said, "Tell me about yourself."

"Is this a job interview?" she snapped. What kind of game was he playing?

"No. You are the most interesting woman I've met in a long time and I want to know all about you."

"At three in the morning?"

He sipped his coffee and settled back against the beige vinyl booth. "What better time? No distractions. I don't know any of the people in your life. You can tell me anything."

And because it was just about the craziest thing she'd ever heard, she did. She told him about growing up near Seattle with a hairdresser mother and a schoolteacher father. How she'd got in with a bad crowd in high school and nearly flunked out. After which she'd left home, worked as a waitress and finally realized she wanted more out of life. So she saved up her money, went to college and got a marketing/PR diploma. Working at the radio station in Elk Crossing had been her big break. Even as she told a virtual stranger about the experience she remembered the excitement of feeling she was finally on her way. She was good at promotions, bursting with ideas and enthusiasm.

The salary at the radio station was pitiful, but she'd seen it as an entry level position, one she knew she could advance from.

Then she discovered the station manager. All he wanted was cheap staff he could push around. He was more interested in how she made coffee than her ideas. She answered the phones, made excuses for him when he wasn't around and the closest she got to running a promotion was the filing cabinet.

By the time she'd quit she was going out with Tyler and it seemed easier simply to stay and find any job at all than to go through all that wasted effort and dashed hopes again. She couldn't quite meet Sadhu's eyes as she told him she'd gone back to being a server.

There was nothing wrong with what she was doing; serving was a respectable profession and she was in the best restaurant in town, but somehow she knew he'd understand how she felt about it. Like she'd given up.

Sadhu listened to her as though her story was the most fascinating thing he'd ever heard.

"What does Tyler do?"

"When his dad passed away, his mom took over the hardware store. He helps her."

He made a strange sound, kind of like a snort.

"What?"

"Nothing. Let's order. I'm starving."

When she thought about it, she was starving, too. And getting jittery from too many fill-ups of coffee. Sadhu ordered Earl's special breakfast, which was three fried eggs, bacon, sausages, pancakes and a small steak.

She settled on waffles.

There was something about sharing breakfast with a man you'd only just met the night before that was intimate. Even though they hadn't had sex, hadn't even kissed, she found herself telling him things she normally kept to herself. Asking him about himself.

It seemed the most natural thing in the world to reach over and snag a piece of bacon off his plate, then sample the steak he held out to her on a fork.

"The atmosphere isn't much at Earl's but the food is good," she said, when she'd eaten as much as she could of the huge crispy waffles. To her everlasting amazement, Sadhu finished his plate. Then finished hers.

"Where do you put all that food?"

He patted his belly. "It's fuel, baby. We're playing the quarterfinals tomorrow." He shook his head. "No. Today. You should come watch."

She should go home and never see this guy again. That's what a smart girl who didn't want her life turned upside down would do. "What time?"

"We play at four. And we don't have too many cheerleaders."

"I'll see what I can do."

By the time they left, the sky was lightening. Even though it was officially morning, she had no desire to go home. She dug out gum from her purse, offered him some and then helped herself on the assumption that they'd soon be kissing and she thought fresh breath would be nice. His eyes gleamed as he popped the gum into his mouth and she figured he was as eager as she was to get to the good stuff.

But again he surprised her.

"The rain's stopped. Let's go back to the lake and watch the sunrise." He took them back the way they'd come.

While they did so, she used every flirtatious tool in her arsenal. Quick little touches, holding his gaze for a second longer than comfortable. She undid her seat belt and turned to face him, pushing her chest forward, so her body language was more like a tirade: *Touch me, kiss me, take me.*

Instead he put on music and talked about his job as a firefighter. Until she was so horny she wanted to climb in his lap and show him exactly what kids in Elk Crossing did when they went parking.

The sunrise was predictably gorgeous, flaming over the mountains and lighting the lake. It wasn't a sight she was around to see very often, but her pleasure was ruined by the very annoying behavior of the man who'd been all over her right up until the moment he got her alone.

When he turned to her and said, "We should probably get back. I have to shower and get to practice," she was at the end of her rope.

Yanking her seat belt on and snapping it with a

vicious click, she wailed, "What do you think you're doing?"

He looked a little embarrassed. Put his head back against the headrest and closed his eyes. "I think I'm playing hard to get."

She was understandably incensed. "Playing hard to get? In the first place, this isn't the fifties, and in the second place, you're a guy!"

He shook his head, looking rueful. "Don't think I don't realize how foolish it sounds. But I like you a lot. And I think you sell yourself too cheaply." He looked over at her and she saw that his dark eyes were serious. "I think you deserve better. You're an amazing woman. Your friends love you. You're beautiful, smart, a lot of fun. So why would you settle? You got a crappy job? Okay. Happens to all of us." He leaned closer. "So, what are you going to do about it?"

"It's not—"

He interrupted her ruthlessly. "You really want to stay with some mama's boy who says he'll meet you and doesn't show up? Are you that woman?"

She shook her head.

"No."

He pointed to her bag. "You want to kill yourself with those cigarettes or are you going to quit?"

"I'm trying, but—"

"No more excuses. I think it's time you start running your life from now on."

"Why are you doing this?" Her voice was barely a whisper. It was hard to speak up against so much truth. It hurt, stung like being outside naked in a hailstorm, but he was right. She knew he was right. When was she going to take charge of her life?

"I'm trying to help."

"You barely know me."

His smile went a little crooked. "I know a woman a lot like you. My sister. She won't listen to me and I can't stand watching her waste her best years. But I think you might listen to me."

"And why might I do that?"

His grin was pure male arrogance. Which, like everything else, looked gorgeous on him. "Because you want in my pants, and you're not getting any until you quit smoking and dump that sack of useless you call your 'sort of boyfriend.'"

She looked as tough as she knew how to look, which wasn't easy when she'd been up all night, hadn't seen a mirror in a while and was pretty sure her mascara was smudged.

"You think I'd change my whole life so I could have sex with you?"

He shrugged in a gesture of pure male arrogance as though he imagined women would do a lot more than change their jobs, dump their boyfriends and quit smoking in order to be with him.

"No idea. Decision's yours, babe. But I hope so."

"I should change my whole life for a guy who's in town for a few days?"

"No. You should change your life because you want to."

Hi picked up her hand, brushed a kiss across the thin, sensitive skin of her inner wrist, sparking a torrent of feeling.

"And I'm in town for four days." He set her hand back in her lap. "A lot can happen in four days."

13

EMILY STRETCHED, FEELING every deliciously satisfied inch of her body purr with sensation. After a night of loving, they'd awakened this morning ravenous for each other.

Jonah, who had just rolled out of bed muttering about being late for his practice, eyed her and from the look on his face only his waiting teammates prevented him from crawling back into bed with her.

She smiled at him. "That should give you some good energy for your games today."

He scratched the stubble on his chin. "Are you kidding? I can't even feel my legs."

She laughed. "I know. I'm actually a plant from the other team, paid a lot of money to seduce you and wear you out before you play."

He chuckled. "You're good at what you do."

"You're pretty good yourself." And wasn't that an understatement. She realized that she hadn't expected a lot of finesse from Jonah. More athleticism and enthusiasm, but when he got between the sheets he was a sensitive and intuitive lover. He seemed to know exactly how and where she liked to be touched, when she wanted to play and be goofy, when she wanted to be serious.

Or maybe they simply connected in a way that made

them understand each other. She didn't really feel like analyzing any of it, only reveling in this strange and very short-lived affair.

"I guess I got my fantasy after all."

"Huh?"

"Sex with a stranger. Number one female fantasy, remember? That's what you told me and you seem like you've done some research."

"I was just throwing the idea out there in case you wanted to use me, that's all." He walked on his way to the bathroom nude and she enjoyed watching his truly excellent butt, the long strong thighs. Mmm.

"And I appreciate it."

He got to the bathroom door and turned. This time giving her a most excellent view of the front of him. Mmm-mmm. "And hey, if you've got any other fantasies you want to explore, I am telling you right now that I am open-minded, pretty athletic." He looked at her, squinting as though reading all the secrets lodged within her. "And not afraid of heights."

And as he disappeared into the bathroom, the corners of his eyes crinkled in amusement, she suddenly pictured the two of them up high. On a Ferris wheel. No, too tame. A roller coaster. Making love while people screamed during the stomach-plunging drop. No, that wasn't going to work. Ooh, one of those treetop canopies in the jungle, the world spread beneath them, their bed a mat of palm leaves. He'd twist his athlete's body to pick ripe fruit from above them. Mango maybe, if it even grew in jungle tops, and he'd peel the fruit, squeeze the juice onto her skin.

Oh, if she didn't get out of bed soon she wasn't getting out.

"What are you up to today?" Jonah asked her when he came out of the shower, this time not bothering with his modesty towel. It was nice to look at him in the daylight.

"Up to?" With a feeling of regret she dragged her gaze away from a body part she'd love to play with all day and tried to marshal her thoughts. "I have a free day today. I'll go for a run, maybe have lunch out with a friend. Then tonight it's the rehearsal dinner. Then the wedding tomorrow and we're all done." With a pang she realized she was checking out on Sunday, back to her real life. Living in the same city as Jonah, but he hadn't said anything about seeing her again once this was over. Maybe he was the one with the sex with a stranger fantasy, and he was quite happy to keep her as a stranger in his life.

His jaw tightened. "Is that fool dentist going to be drooling all over you at the dinner?"

"Cousin Buddy? I don't know. I hope not. I think you freaked him out last night being so big and tough and scary."

"Lots of people get nervous around cops. He was real spooked, though. Probably has a drawerful of unpaid parking tickets. Or he owes back taxes." He shrugged, but the puzzled frown remained. "What was all that ruckus about when he came out of the bathroom?"

"Ruckus?" She wrinkled her brow trying to remember. "Oh, I picked up his cell phone by mistake. Thought it was mine. He got all bent out of shape like I was taking his calls or something."

"A guy shouldn't leave his cell phone lying around in a bar if he doesn't want people making that kind of mistake."

She nodded. "I'm glad you reminded me of that. I saw a text message. I'd forgotten all about it. It said something about everything being set for pickup at midnight on Saturday."

"What's he picking up at midnight?"

"I don't know. But Saturday's tomorrow, the night Leanne and Derek are getting married. Do you think he's got some infantile prank in mind?"

"Most likely."

"Can you arrest him for inappropriate behavior?"

He showed his teeth. "I'd love an excuse to put that little schmuk behind bars. But it's not my jurisdiction." He dug through his bag, pulled out briefs and jeans. "You know, there's something about that guy that doesn't feel right."

"Cop's instincts?"

He shrugged. "Don't knock them. It can't hurt to do some quiet checking. Find out why Cousin Buddy gets so nervous when he meets a cop."

He grabbed the pad of hotel stationery off the desk and the blue plastic pen with Elk Crossing Lodge written in gold down the side punctuated by a tiny gold Elk logo. Clicked open the ballpoint. "What's Buddy's real name?"

Luckily, her aunt had mentioned it in passing. *His name's really Bruce, but when he was a little boy they had a dog called Buddy and little Brucie got confused and thought it was his name. He's been Buddy ever since.* "His real name's Bruce." And she gave him the correct spelling for her cousin's last name, which he jotted down.

"What else do you know about Buddy? Tell me everything."

She told him everything she knew about her third

cousin, which was surprisingly a lot given how much her family had been extolling his attributes. *Thirty-four and not married, so you know he's ready to settle down with the right woman.* "He's thirty-four."

His practice is in Boise. He could have gone for a cheaper rent in an outlying medical center, but Buddy's one for doing everything the best. He's right downtown in the medical center. He's smart, too. Do you know he graduated third in his class from Penn Dental School? He drives a Porsche.

It was surprising how much she'd learned as her family tried to sell her on her third cousin. After she'd recalled as many details as she could, she said, "This isn't going to be embarrassing to us, is it?"

"No. I'm only asking a few questions from some colleagues, all nice and quiet. So long as he's not a wanted fugitive he'll never know anybody was asking. Like I say, it's probably nothing, but you get to my age and you learn to listen to your gut."

"Good. I'm glad this is all unofficial. He's a strange one. But then so are most of my family."

She rose to sitting, watching him dress. "Any chance you can make the rehearsal dinner tonight? That would stop Buddy drooling over me."

He paused to glance up at her. "When and where?"

"Dino's Italian Restaurant. The wedding rehearsal's at five. Dinner at seven."

"I might be a bit late, but I should make dinner okay."

She was much happier about this news than she should have been. She told herself it was because Jonah by her side meant an absent Buddy, but the truth was she enjoyed having him around. Liked the sexual sizzle between them, his no-nonsense way of looking at the world, and the way he made her laugh. She was definitely going to enjoy him for the last couple of days—and nights—they had together.

He kissed her on his way out the door. "See you later."

She did some yoga stretches, savoring the entire day to herself. No errands to run, no more decorations to make, nothing to do but enjoy herself. Her cell phone rang.

"Hello?"

"The cake is ready to be picked up today," her mother said, bubbling with excitement at the thought.

"Really?" She recalled her conversation with Jonah and how right he was. He barely knew her and he'd noticed that her family took advantage of her single status and inability to say no. She had to start standing up for herself and saying no once in a while. *No.* She mouthed the word silently. *No.* She would not pick up the cake. Enough was enough. She gripped her phone a little tighter as though that might help her determination.

"Your uncle was going to drive to the bakery and get it, but he and your aunt have a million things to do. I told them you wouldn't mind."

"But—" So much for saying no. She hadn't even been asked. She'd been told.

"They said I must be so proud to have a daughter like you, and I told them I am."

See? If Jonah could hear her mother on the phone he'd understand why she was such a pushover. Now what was she supposed to do? If she refused to get the cake her mother would look foolish. Besides, her aunt and uncle must have a million things to do, and since she'd done all the calligraphy on the cards they'd let her off from decorating the hall.

She sighed, releasing her death grip on her cell. "What time will the cake be ready?"

"Ten o'clock. And did Leanne remind you about the hairdo rehearsal?"

"What hairdo rehearsal?" she asked, getting a bad feeling in her scalp.

"You know, the hairdo rehearsal, so all the bridesmaids match. It's at Gilda's Salon at noon."

She sighed. So much for lunch with a friend. So much for at least wearing her own hairstyle with that hideous dress. Glancing at her watch she realized she didn't even have time for a very long run. It was hell being the reliable one.

JONAH MADE A COUPLE OF CALLS on his way to the rink. The kind of calls that don't get logged. No reports are generated. Nothing official ever takes place and information quietly gets exchanged.

He got to the rink and was putting on his skates when Sadhu came in yawning. His hair was all on end, he was heavy-eyed from lack of sleep and it was pretty clear he'd just rolled out of bed. Not his own, Jonah guessed.

"Don't tell me, Kirsten and you spent some quality time together."

He grinned. "I never talk about my conquests. You know that." After the raucous comments and laughter died down, he added, "She likes waffles for breakfast. That's all I'm saying."

"You dog. Hope you got some strength left in you to play."

He took a long look at Jonah. "Old man, you worry about your own strength."

EMILY SET OFF AT A SLOW JOG, heading for the park. She passed bundled-up kids on swings and slides, mothers chatting to each other, their hands wrapped around take-out coffees. The rain had knocked a lot of the fall leaves from the trees, and they squished beneath her feet as she ran, sending up the smell of autumn. The bright reds and oranges and yellows still hung from the oaks and maples, flaming against a leaden sky.

She ran on, taking it easy because she was tired, and most of the night had been a workout. She smiled at the memories. Who knew a tough guy cop could be so inventive?

Her phone rang as she hit her stride. She glanced at it and saw it was her mother. She should ignore the call. It was bound to be something that would annoy her. But it was her mother and she always had the guilty fear that the one time she ignored her mom would be the time the woman who gave her life was in mid heart attack, on her last gasp, and she could have saved her if only...

"Hello?"

"You sound out of breath. Is everything all right?"

"I'm running."

"Oh, running. Nice for you to be able to take a vacation when we're all killing ourselves over this wedding. I've personally hung fifty paper roses already this morning."

Guilt washed over her, but she knew it wasn't really the unfair accusation that she wasn't pulling her weight, it was the primeval fear that her mother could somehow divine what she'd been up to all night.

"I'll be there at noon for the hair rehearsal. And I'm picking up the cake on the way."

"Good. But I'm calling about rental dishes."

"Rental dishes?" It was no good. She couldn't jog and talk at the same time, so she stopped and walked over to a big old oak tree, leaning against the solid trunk. It was damp, and cool through her running pants, but she didn't care. "What about the rental dishes?"

She should have known her mother wasn't having a heart attack, and even if she was, she was surrounded by family all hanging paper roses Emily had twisted, and twinkle lights, and propping the place cards she'd personally calligraphied onto the tables. Her heavy breathing slowed.

"I need you to pick them up."

"But, Mom, I'm already picking up the cake."

"I know. That's why I thought of you. Morton's Rentals is on your way."

Just say no, she reminded herself. "Isn't there somebody else who could do it?"

"Of course, don't give it another thought. I'll get Leanne to pick them up. She won't be busy. She's got nothing better to do."

"Not Leanne. I was thinking—"

"Or me. I'm nearly sixty and my sciatica's murder

in this weather, and I've spent the morning hanging paper roses so you could have the day off, but don't give it a thought. I will get the dishes, and your father with his bad back can help me. Go back to your running."

It was hopeless. Why did she even bother? "Where do you want the dishes dropped off?"

She turned her phone off then, with a vicious jab. Whoever wanted to talk to her, she didn't want to talk to them.

Of course, now Jonah would phone and want to talk dirty in her ear and instead he'd get her voice mail. It was all so unfair.

She picked up her pace, running her frustrations out until she was drenched with sweat and panting. She stopped to stretch out her muscles and then headed in for a quick shower.

She was just drying off when the room phone rang. She considered ignoring it in case it was her mother again, but curiosity got the better of her. "Hello?"

"I need to talk to you," a breathless voice said in a whisper.

"Who is this?"

"Kirsten."

"Kirsten? Where are you?"

"In the lobby."

"I just got out of the shower."

"Perfect. I can talk to you while you get ready."

She managed to scramble into her clothes before the knock sounded on the door. She opened it to find Kirsten looking a little the worse for wear, in last night's clothes. Her makeup had worn off, her hair was a mess and she was pale from lack of sleep.

All the symptoms of a man-crush.

"Sadhu?"

A grumpy-looking nod answered her. "I need you to cover for me. When I got home this morning, Tyler's truck was parked outside my place so I made Sadhu drop me off here. You were out, so I had some coffee in the restaurant. Where were you?"

"I went for a run."

"Oh. Nice. I should take up running. I really need to get back in shape."

She looked stunned, not so much like a woman who'd had raunchy sex all night, but like a woman who'd had a life-changing experience.

But then Emily thought about her night with Jonah and realized a night of raunchy sex probably could be life-changing.

Kirsten looked at her with those big brown innocent puppy eyes. "I'm going to tell Tyler that I had too much to drink and came home and crashed in your room. He doesn't know about Jonah, so he'd figure it was a girls-only slumber party. Okay?"

And just like that, another favor was being asked of her. She should definitely say no to this one. She didn't like lying for one thing, and was terrible at it for another.

"I'm not sure—"

"Oh, Em, I don't know what I'm doing." And with that, Kirsten flopped onto the bed on her back. "Last night was the most amazing night of my life."

Emily put her hand up. "Okay, I might lie for you, but I really don't want to hear about your sex life."

The woman bounced up and crossed her legs on top

of the quilt. "What sex life?" she almost yelled. "I didn't have sex with Sadhu. It was more like an all-night counseling session."

"Sadhu? He looked ready to eat you up with a spoon."

"I know. That's what I thought." She rolled off the bed and went to the in-room coffeemaker. "You get ready. I'll make coffee while we talk."

She went into the bathroom and filled the carafe with water, came back and started the maker going. Emily dried her hair. This room simply wasn't big enough for all the activity it was seeing.

"What's with the curtain?" her unwanted guest asked when she'd turned off the blow-dryer.

"Go and look."

Kirsten drew back the curtain and laughed. "No way. It's like camping. Without the campfire and marshmallows." Letting the curtain drop, she poured them both coffee, went to her bag and drew out a battered pack of cigarettes.

"You can't smoke in here."

"I know. I'm giving them to you. Can you please hold on to them for me?"

"You want me to hold your cigarettes? Why?"

"No. I don't." She snatched the pack back, closed her eyes, and opened them again. "Yes. I do." She drew one from the package. "I'll keep this one, for emergencies. No. Not for emergencies. So I can enjoy my last cigarette. I think I'll smoke it someplace special. I'll take my time, enjoy every moment of it, and then I'll always be able to remember my last smoke."

Emily took the pack and placed it inside the desk

drawer. "You sound a little like a crazy person, but I think it's great that you're quitting."

"Me, too."

She pushed her hair behind her ears and dug around in her bag. "I need gum." She found the pack, pushed a piece into her mouth and chewed like it was the first meal she'd seen in weeks and she was starving. "I've never craved a cigarette when I was smoking as much as I do now that I've decided to quit. It's like when you go on a diet and all you can think about is food." She chomped harder.

"Maybe you should think about the patch?"

She watched Kirsten chew, adding a new piece to the wad in her mouth long before she could have lost the flavor in the first piece. She couldn't help but compare the jittery behavior of her friend with her own almost Zen-like calmness induced by a night of amazing sex.

Interesting.

"When I left Brandy's last night I figured you and Sadhu were going to, you know, have amazing sex all night."

Another piece of gum came out of the bag and she stuffed it into her mouth. Soon she wouldn't be able to talk at all. "Ha," she said around the gum. "I wish." And scowled.

She looked so put out, like a little kid contemplating a temper tantrum, that Emily couldn't help but smile. "So, you spent the entire night with a hot guy and didn't get laid."

"Stop rubbing it in."

"Was it because of Tyler?" Emily was all for being faithful, but Tyler and Kirsten had always had one of those relationships where you felt as though they were both hanging out together until something better came along. She knew Kirsten was well aware that she wasn't the only one Tyler saw, so she doubted that it was some kind of loyalty keeping her from doing the deed with a new man.

"No." Then she put her head on one side. "Actually, maybe in a way." She chewed for a bit and then with a huff, pulled the wad of gum out of her mouth and tossed it in the wastepaper bin. "I'm going to have to tell you everything."

Emily glanced at the clock beside the bed. It was almost eleven. She really hoped the story didn't take too long since she still needed to pick up the cake, the rental dishes and get to the hair salon by noon.

She got her makeup bag out and started on her face while Kirsten talked, but a couple of times she had to kick-start herself back to the task because the story pouring out of Kirsten was so incredible.

Sadhu should have been a one-night stand. He had one-night lover written all over him. And instead he'd taken a pass on sleeping with a woman who was not only beautiful, but sexy and willing. Not only that, he'd said some things to her that were making her think. He'd said what Emily and Leanne and Kirsten's other friends had been thinking, hinting or outright telling her for months. Maybe from the right person, the message was finally seeping through.

Maybe there was more to Sadhu than she'd realized.

At the end of the recital, Kirsten didn't look any happier. In fact, she appeared so confused that Emily wanted to hug her. She didn't. Even though she wasn't in town that often, she'd often been sorry to see Kirsten still in a town that was a great place to raise a family, a charming place to retire, but a dead end for someone like her. Instead of getting out when the job hadn't worked out, she'd slid. Professionally, personally and, Emily suspected where Tyler was concerned, sexually.

Now a man had entered her life, however briefly, who had decided to provoke her out of her rut. Emily had no idea what his motives might be or whether Kirsten was ready to move forward with her life, but she liked the possibility.

"So here I am. And I don't know what to do."

Emily rose, grabbed her bag and coat. "I'm going to drive you home. Once you get there, I suggest a shower and a change of clothes. Then why don't you think about what you want? Sadhu saw some things after knowing you only a few hours. Maybe he's right, maybe he isn't. Nobody can figure that out but you."

"Did you hear the part when he said he's playing hard to get?"

She suppressed a smile with an effort. "That was my favorite part."

"Guys never play hard to get. I don't think it's in their genetic code."

"I admit, it's a new one on me. It must have been kind of nice, though, to spend a whole night talking."

Kirsten gathered her things and they left the room together. "Some of it was." She stopped stock-still in the middle of the corridor. "I didn't even get a kiss."

"No!" Emily opened her mouth in profound shock. "That tease."

"Oh, yeah, it's funny for you. I know you and Jonah weren't talking all night long. You have no idea what sexual frustration feels like."

"Sure I do. Not this morning, but I've definitely experienced the phenomenon. You have to think he's experiencing it, too."

Kirsten suddenly looked happier than she had since she first burst in on Emily. "You think?"

"Sure. Look at it from his point of view. You're sexy, gorgeous, were dressed like that, he spent all night with you and he didn't even get a kiss."

An evil-sounding chuckle came from beside her.

"See what I mean? He may have acted cool, but I bet he needed a long, cold shower this morning."

"Good."

"So, I'll see you at the wedding rehearsal tonight?"

"Um, maybe earlier."

Kirsten wasn't a bridesmaid, so Emily didn't imagine she'd be at the salon at noon. "Is there another prewedding event I'm not aware of?" The possibilities were terrifying. An expedition in the forest to pick fall foliage. A prenuptial demolition derby, perhaps.

"No, but…" She let out an anguished breath. "I'm thinking of going to the rink to watch the Paters play. I wondered if you'd come with me."

"Really?"

"Yeah. I figure you must go all the time and this way it wouldn't seem so obvious if I showed up."

In fact Emily had never been to watch Jonah play hockey. But she kind of liked the idea. Except that this had the potential to be awkward.

"What time are they playing today?"

"Four."

"Right. I guess we could go for an hour or so on our way to the dinner."

"Awesome. Pick me up?"

She shrugged. "Why not." Then she turned her head. "What about Tyler? Isn't he coming to the rehearsal dinner with you? Won't it be kind of strange to go watch the guys play hockey and then have to ditch Sadhu?"

"No. I don't think Tyler's coming to the dinner tonight." She took a deep breath. Nodded. "In fact, I'm sure of it."

14

THERE WAS A TEXT MESSAGE on Jonah's cell phone when he came off the ice after practice.

Call me. Emily.

Not the sexiest message he'd ever been texted, but it still gave him a nice jolt to see her name there on his phone. He found a quiet spot and called her.

"Hey, sexy," he said when she answered.

"Hi. Can you hang on a second? I'm going outside."

"Sure. Maybe we can talk dirty."

But he didn't think she even heard him. There was some kind of din going on, a lot of high-pitched voices talking at once and machinery noise.

"Okay. Sorry about that."

"Where are you?"

"Hairdresser. And I do not want to hear one word from you about my hair when I see you. Okay?"

"You have beautiful hair."

"Not today. Let's just say my hair now matches that dress."

"Unless it's a pumpkin stalk with a single green leaf, not possible."

She chuckled. "Okay, real reason I'm calling. Have you seen Sadhu?"

"Yeah. Why?"

"He's really done a number on Kirsten. She wants to come watch your game."

"Look, Sadhu's a good buddy of mine but he does a number on a lot of women. She seems like a nice girl, but I don't think she should get her hopes up."

"He asked her to come watch the game."

"He did?"

"Yeah. Unusual behavior?"

"Totally. Huh." He realized that Sadhu had seemed more pleased with himself than usual today. Interesting. Even more interesting that Emily was playing chaperone. Was she checking out that he wanted her there? "So, you're coming to support the team."

"That's what I want to talk to you about. You'll have to tell them that I'm pretending to be your girlfriend. I can't have the truth getting out to my family."

He grinned, glad she couldn't see him. "Emily, we are men. We do not gossip like women. If the guys see you here they'll be cool."

He could hear street noises from her cell phone. Pictured her standing outside a salon somewhere, probably rolling her eyes. "They won't know me. They'll try and introduce themselves and we'll be busted," she explained slowly as though he might have taken a few too many pucks to the head. She had a point.

"Okay. I'll tell them you have Obsessive Compulsive Disorder and can't shake hands. How's that?"

"Less than helpful."

"Come on, Em. I'll figure something out."

"I probably shouldn't come."

"You should definitely come. I'm all excited now at the thought of seeing you. You can't let me down." He sounded like he was joking, but mostly he wasn't. He really did want to see her. It had been hours. He could still picture her as she'd been that morning, naked and rumpled, a satiated smile on her face and whisker burn on lots of rarely seen parts of her body.

He shifted, knowing his uniform would no longer fit him if he didn't redirect his thoughts. But it didn't seem to matter. His thoughts were on a one-way street. "I hope you can eat dinner fast."

"Why?"

"Because I'm planning to take you home early tonight."

She chuckled, low and earthy. "Didn't you get your fill last night?"

"Darlin', I barely even got started. Last night was getting-to-know-you sex."

She snorted. "I think we know each other pretty well now."

"Exactly. So we can move on to the more advanced stage of our relationship."

"Already? After one night?" She sounded intrigued, also excited.

"We're both quick studies. Why not? There must be something you've always wanted to try out. Something racy that yours truly would be happy to provide."

"Well, I know you said you'd be willing to fulfill any fantasy."

He gulped. "Uh-huh. I remember."

"I do have this fantasy."

He damn near fell off his skates. He wobbled his

way over to a bench and sat down heavily. He'd been toying with her. He could spend days in bed—and on any other surface he could think of—with this woman and not have to stretch for new ideas. But if she had a fantasy, he'd do his best to make it happen. "Yeah? Tell me about it."

"It's kind of embarrassing."

"My favorite kind."

"Well, I'm in a hotel room. In bed."

"Good start. What are you wearing?"

"A little black see-through number." Her voice was low, teasing. He hadn't realized how much he loved her voice; he'd been distracted by the rest of her, but now that all he had was her voice he definitely noticed. It was low-pitched, musical. A hint of devilry in her tone.

"Are you still there?" she asked. And he realized he'd been so busy imagining her in that black see-through number that he'd forgotten to speak.

"Black. Black is good."

"I'm ready for bed when there's a knock on the door."

"No. Are you expecting anyone?"

"That's the strangest part. I'm not." She sounded a little breathless now. And he recalled the way she'd sung, as though she'd done a lot of it in her time, and then Leanne telling him that she'd been in the musical theater program in high school. Obviously, she'd done some acting as well as singing.

"Do you answer the door?"

"Well, first I tiptoe to the door and peek out the peephole thing."

"Good plan. Um, does your black nightie ride up when you do that?"

"Oh, definitely."

"I'm getting a visual. Go on."

"Are you skating while we're talking?"

He couldn't even have stood. "No."

"Oh, you sound out of breath. I thought maybe you were working out."

"Only my imagination. So, you're looking out the peephole, your black see-through negligee riding up over your butt."

"Yes. And who do you think is there?"

"A studly hockey player?"

She made a sound like a quiet chuckle, then stifled it. "No. A room service waiter."

"Well, a guy can hope."

"He has one of those rolling carts that room service people use. I can see the stainless steel dome they use over the plates, and there's a vase with a single red rose."

Did a woman ever have a fantasy that didn't involve a single red rose? He wanted to mention it, but decided he might throw her off this very interesting track.

"Do you open the door?"

"Of course. I don't want the food to get cold. So I let him in and tell him he must have the wrong room."

"And?"

"And he looks at me for a long time. He's very good-looking. When he stares at my chest, I realize I've forgotten to put on my robe."

"Doesn't sound like you at all."

"Anyway, he says we'd better eat while it's still hot. He takes the rose out of the water and runs the petals over my breasts. And then he takes the silver lid off the plate and—"

She sucked in a breath and in an entirely different voice said, "Damn." Then, he heard "Yes, I'm out here. Of course I don't smoke. I needed to make a call." The echo of a female voice followed. No doubt a lovely woman, but one he'd cheerfully strangle right now. Then Emily again. "Sorry. I've got to go."

"But what's under the dome?"

"I'll see you at four."

It was several minutes before he was fit to move. As he took his place back on the ice, he couldn't stop wondering what was under that silver dome.

THE OVER-THIRTY MEN'S LEAGUE would never be confused with NHL Hockey, Emily realized when she and Kirsten entered the rink later that day. They were both dressed for the rehearsal dinner, and though she'd brushed out her hair, it still insisted on curling in ringlets.

As they walked into the cavernous space she felt completely overdressed.

There was nothing slick or commercial about this space; it was an old-time arena. The rink, hard wooden benches tiering up to the rafters. The air was chilly and smelled a little stale, as if too many skates had been aired out and too little fresh air let in.

The fan base was also much smaller than she'd seen on the few occasions when she'd watched a professional hockey game. Clusters of people sat around the bleachers, wives and families she guessed, and some local hockey fans.

"You made it." They turned and Sadhu was striding toward them in his uniform, all but his skates and helmet, both of which he carried. His grin was wide and rakish. He looked at Kirsten and even though he said, "You made it," somehow she felt as though he was saying, *I want to see you naked*.

Kirsten obviously received the same message for she giggled and said, "We came to see what you've got."

"Cool."

Kirsten took a breath. She looked fresh and pretty, obviously she'd found time for a nap. "And, I wanted to ask you to be my date tonight for the wedding rehearsal dinner."

Sadhu looked up quickly. "What about Tyler?"

"Tyler and I are history."

"Then I'd be delighted to be your date. What time shall I pick you up?"

Jonah came up behind him. He didn't say anything at first, but the way he was looking at Emily, she was getting a clear *I want to see you naked* signal from him, too. The cool air seemed to sizzle up around them.

While Kirsten and Sadhu talked together in low voices, Jonah led her a few steps away and leaned in to whisper in her ear. She smelled the workout on his skin and in his hair. "What's under the dome?"

It took her a second to figure out what he was talking about and then remembered the fantasy she'd shared.

She pulled back far enough to see the devil lights dancing in his eyes. "I really got you on that one, didn't I?"

"Are you kidding? I can't even skate in a straight line."

"What's under the dome changes with my mood. Use your imagination."

He groaned. "I can't stop."

15

"EVENING, JONAH," THE HOTEL manager greeted him.

"Hi." He walked up close, checked the lobby of the Elk Crossing Lodge to make sure no one else could hear him and said, "Listen, I need a favor."

If the man was surprised, he'd been in the hospitality business long enough not to show it. "Of course. Anything in my power for one of our valued customers."

"I need to borrow one of your waiter's uniforms."

"A waiter's uniform. And this would be for a costume party?"

"Yes. So glad you understood right away. Also, a tray and one of those silver dome things you put over the room service dishes."

"Well…"

"You'd get it back. And I'll have the uniform dry-cleaned before I return it."

The man scratched his balding head. "That's not necessary, we have a laundry service here. But it's a little unorthodox." He glanced at Jonah as though figuring correctly that he wasn't planning to moonlight as a waiter.

"Look. I'm a cop. I promise you I won't use it for anything you wouldn't like."

A pair of shrewd eyes surveyed him. And then he nodded. Jonah was certain that the bedbug situation and how easygoing he'd been definitely played in his favor. "I'll see what I can do. When do you need it for?"

"Tonight."

"I see. Anything else?"

"Well, since you ask. Is there an extra room still available?"

"Yes. Of course, I'll have it prepared immediately."

"Thanks. I only need it for tonight."

"It's our pleasure to serve you. You've been so understanding about the little problem we had earlier in the week that I'm willing to bend the rules a little."

"Really appreciate it. I'll be down later."

"Come directly to me. I'll be here all evening."

Emily seemed a little worked up with all the wedding events, nerves and the usual snafus. From experience he knew well that the wedding day would be a busy and possibly stressful one for the bridesmaid. What she needed was a good dose of relaxation tonight. And she'd given him exactly the way to relax her.

EMILY WAS GLAD JONAH HAD forgotten his jacket at the restaurant. He'd gone back for it, which should give her a good twenty minutes to herself. And she knew exactly what she'd do.

Stripping and stepping into a terry robe, she wrapped her hair in a towel turban, warmed the clay mask she'd brought with her under a hot tap, then squeezed the thick, greeny-gray contents onto her fingers and spread the luscious mud onto her face.

Bringing the rest of the things over to the bed, she squeezed the special cream mask for hands and feet onto her feet first, then slipped them into cotton socks and then the plastic bags provided in the kit. She then rubbed the sticky mess into her hands, sliding them into cotton gloves and more plastic. With a sigh, she lay back on the pillow and drifted. Fifteen minutes and she'd be done. With luck she'd be unmasked and dried off before Jonah returned.

Maybe she was being forced to wear the ugliest bridesmaid dress ever, with bad hair, but at least her skin would be radiant.

It had been a good evening, she thought. Buddy had settled himself as far from Jonah as he could get, which was excellent. Her parents and family had liked Jonah, she could tell, and he'd fit in with her friends. But the most fun of the evening had been watching Kirsten and Sadhu. It was as though they were both trying out a relationship from the opposite of the way they usually did it. And this made them a little awkward around each other.

She found them sweet. Where last night she'd been so sure they'd be in bed together within hours of meeting—which hadn't happened—tonight she wasn't sure.

Jonah and her she was sure of, though. The way he'd been sending her steamy glances over the all-you-can-eat Italian buffet, the entire evening had been foreplay.

She was in that twilight zone between waking and sleep when someone knocked on the door. She ignored it. Jonah had a key and everyone else needed to learn to call first.

The knock was repeated. Louder this time and more insistent. Irked, she opened her eyes.

"Who is it?" she called out.

"Room service," a gruff voice yelled through the door.

"Wrong room."

A pause.

"This is room 318."

"Yes, but I didn't order room service." She was getting irritated from all the yelling. "Go back to the kitchen and check."

There was a pause.

"Lady, would you open the damn door?"

Her eyes flew open once more and she turned her head, feeling the drying mud start to crack. Not only had that last comment been very unprofessional, but the voice had sounded awfully familiar. "Jonah?"

"Use the peephole." He sounded absolutely peeved and in that second she remembered the silly fantasy she'd woven for him.

She struggled off the bed and squished her way to the door.

She looked through the peephole and there was Jonah, looking big, embarrassed and adorable in a waiter's uniform. He'd even found some white cotton gloves from somewhere. In his hands was a tray containing a bud vase with a single red rose, a plate covered with a silver dome, a silver bucket containing a bottle of champagne, and two glasses.

"Oh, Jonah," she said softly.

"Can I come in?"

"I just need a minute."

"But everything will get cold," he said, sounding exasperated.

"Don't move," she cried and sped to the bathroom, tossing bags as she went.

She tissued her hands off like the instructions said, but it was too slow and they were sticky. Knowing this was one expensive treatment basically down the drain, she turned on the hot tap and got the soap. She washed her hands, then her feet, going at top speed knowing Jonah was standing outside the door waiting.

Finally, she slapped water on her face to rinse off the mask and dried her face as fast as she could. She pulled the towel off her hair as she ran into the bedroom. Dug through her lingerie until she found something black. It wasn't see-through, it was a very nice Victoria's Secret short black nightgown, but it would have to do. Brush through her hair.

She ran to the door and opened it.

"Yes?"

JONAH LOOKED AT EMILY and gulped. Her face looked like copper that had been left in the rain. Green streaks ran down her temples and striped the sides of her hair. A big patch of gray-green goop was lodged beneath her ear, as though she'd been patched.

Her gown was inside out, and he suspected backward since the tag was staring at him.

A squish of something that looked like white glue seeped between two of her toes.

She was about the cutest thing he'd ever seen.

"Room service," he said.

"You have the wrong room." She was the only woman he could imagine who could pull off haughty while wearing green goop on her neck.

"I don't think so." He shut the door behind him. Placed the tray down on the desk since the bed was a bit of a mess, with a green-streaked towel laid over the pillow, and a couple of used plastic bags tossed on top.

"I, uh—" He thought he was supposed to do the rose next, but he wasn't absolutely certain.

She gave a shriek and that's when he knew she'd caught sight of herself in the mirror. "Wait." She flapped her hands. "Wait. This isn't working at all. I was giving myself a mud mask. I'm a mess," she wailed. "Now the whole fantasy's ruined."

He glanced at her, her body a feast for his eyes, the short gown only teasing him. "No. It isn't."

He dug the key of his temporary room out of his pocket. "Go down the hall to 310. I'll be there in ten minutes." He kissed her shoulder. "We'll start over."

"Really?"

"Really. And this time I hope nobody who sees me in the hall orders anything."

She ran into the bathroom and took a wet cloth to her face. Laughed, delighted. "Did they really?"

He nodded. "Double cheeseburger and fries. I had to call it down to the kitchen. Now some other waiter will get my tip."

"I'll give you an extra good one."

Once she'd cleaned all the green stuff off her, she slipped a raincoat over her gown and stepped into black pumps. Trust Emily to color coordinate her nightdress with her shoes even when no one would see them.

She took the key and slipped out of the room.

SHE LAY ON THE BED, HER short black silk gown riding high on her thighs, the crisp white sheets cool beneath her body.

There was a knock on the door.

She went to the peephole. The room service waiter gave her the stink eye.

She opened up right away.

"Room service." And he pushed his way into the room and shut the door looking harassed. "Kirsten's knocking on your door at this very minute. Luckily the light's not very bright or she'd have figured out it was me."

"Kirsten? What can she want?"

"I don't know, but whatever it is, it can wait until tomorrow."

"Poor Kirsten. That Sadhu has her tangled in knots."

"I know somebody else who is tangled in knots," he informed her. "And I have a special dish for you that needs to be served hot."

His eyes scorched her as he said the words. Kirsten, the wedding, the rental dishes, the bad bridesmaid dress, the list of responsibilities she had for tomorrow, all of them faded away.

"Then we'd better get started right now."

She felt a little breathless as he looked at her with those hard cop eyes that had seen it all. The white jacket and black pants with the stripe down the side, the white shirt and bow tie, none of it was Jonah. He was like a stranger, only a wonderfully familiar one. She found her gaze going to the silver dome.

"What have you brought me to eat?"

"Something sweet and delicious."

She licked her lips. "I never said what was under there. In my fantasy."

"No. I had to improvise."

He set the tray down on the desk that was like the one in their room only clear of junk. None of their stuff was in this room. Jonah must have put his clothes away in the drawer for she couldn't even see his discarded things. She'd have liked to, simply for the familiarity.

This was uncomfortably impersonal. Like her fantasy, but with an edge of unpredictability she wasn't sure she liked. The thing with fantasy was that she was in complete control, changing anything and everything at will. But with Jonah involved, the control had shifted away from her. She wished quite suddenly that she'd never teased him with her silly fantasy.

Certainly she'd never dreamed he'd act it out. At least not without her help.

He reached toward the tray. Slowly. His arm not his in that unfamiliar jacket, the white glove seeming oddly menacing. She was aware of the sounds coming from outside. A vehicle pulling into the gravel parking area. A car door slamming.

He didn't go for the silver dome. His hand closed over the rose.

Slowly he pulled it from the vase, and she saw the water droplets tumble off the dark green stem to splash onto the napkin folded beside the champagne bucket.

The red petals touched the skin of her upper chest and she was shocked by the coolness of the petals, the velvety sweep over her extra sensitive skin. He traced a path across the top of her breasts, over the top, onto the silk, and then ran the flower across the fullest part of her breasts, bringing her nipples tingling to life.

He placed the rose on the bedside table.

"Sit down," he said, gesturing to the bed.

She did. Wondering what was in store. Excited and

apprehensive all at once. How well did she even know this man? Maybe it was the white gloves but she flashed to *Dexter*, the show about a seemingly normal guy—also in law enforcement now she thought about it—who was also a serial killer.

She knew she was being ridiculous. If he'd just take off that silver dome and let her see what he'd brought her—because somehow she was pretty sure it wasn't a roast beef dinner—then she could settle.

As though he'd read her mind, he leaned forward, brushed his lips softly across hers. "Wondering what's under there?"

"Yes."

He nibbled her lower lip. "You can trust me," he whispered.

"I know."

He kissed her for a while, as though he couldn't tear himself away from her mouth. She didn't even care what was under that dome, all she wanted was him, out of that uniform and naked. Preferably now.

But he pulled away at last and she had the satisfaction of seeing his dark pants seriously distended by his erection as he crossed to the room service tray.

He brought the plate with the silver dome over to her. Presented it and with a flourish, removed the lid.

There were two items on the plate. A dish of red, ripe strawberries.

And a black blindfold.

Her gaze flew to his. He was looking at her with challenge, as well as understanding in his eyes. "I figured the basic fantasy was sex with a stranger. So, I took a poll of the guys on the team."

"You did?"

"You'd be surprised at the breadth of experience on an over-thirty hockey team."

"I can't even imagine."

He flicked her a wicked glance. "I talked to most of the other teams, too, to get a good cross section of opinion on what would have been on the tray in your fantasy."

Sure he had. "You did?"

"Mmm-hmm. Some of the guys had some ideas that were a little crude, to be honest with you. And I don't know where you'd buy the equipment in this town."

She swallowed, not at all certain how she felt about the blindfold. "That's a problem."

"Oh, yeah. I thought about asking your aunt and uncle at dinner. They seem like they know Elk Crossing pretty well. But it's hard to work nipple clamps into dinner conversation."

"I admire your restraint."

"Thank you. Then me and some of the guys thought that maybe you'd more easily believe I was a stranger if you couldn't see me." He fingered the black fabric. "Of course, it's all about trust."

"And I could simply pull off the blindfold at any time."

"Theoretically, if you weren't handcuffed."

Her eyes flew wide-open. "Tell me you don't have handcuffs hidden in that ice bucket?" He was a cop. He must have cuffs. Oh, what had she got herself into?

He shook his head. "Without the nipple clamps and so on, I don't see much point in handcuffs."

More relieved than she cared to admit, she agreed that handcuffs on their own were simply too tame.

He picked up the black fabric, ran it up her thigh,

over her body, brushing past her breasts. She felt her breath quicken, and then he slipped the black silk over her eyes, and tied the length gently behind her head.

16

She hadn't been blindfolded since Pin the Tail on the Donkey at a kids' birthday party.

This was quite different.

Without her eyesight, she was super aware of sound, and smell and touch. The muted sounds of the heating system in the hotel, the fragrance of the rose, much more muted than a true summer rose, but smelling of florist's greenery and a slight hint of summer. The sheets had the crisp freshness of laundered linen where the fabric touched her, while everywhere else she was covered by the silky nightdress, giving her an entirely different sensation. Even the blindfold itself was an experience. The fabric had been cool when he first placed it over her eyes, but it was rapidly warming and if she moved her head on the pillow, she could make out the bump of the knot.

A crinkle of foil, the winching sound of untwisting wire, and then the scrape of cork against bottle preceded the pop as he opened the champagne. She heard the hissing sound as he poured the foaming liquid into the glasses, the familiar sounds telling her as clearly as her eyes would have what he was up to.

She heard nothing more and so jumped when a finger pad traced its way down her shoulder, hooking under a strap and pulling it over her shoulder.

He put an arm behind her back and raised her to sitting, then she felt the cool glass touch her lower lip. She was perfectly capable of holding the glass for herself, but it was much more fun to let him feed her. A tiny waterfall of bubbles spilled into her mouth, a little bit escaping to slide over her lip and down her chin. Jonah kissed her wet mouth and then followed the drip of champagne with his tongue.

The wet heat of him licking her, the sizzle of the drink going down her throat, the fact that he was bringing her fantasy to life in an entirely unexpected way, all was making her so hot she could barely keep still. She wanted to crawl all over him, to speed things up and get to the hot sex part, but she restrained herself, feeling pretty certain that her patience would be well rewarded.

"Open your mouth."

She did, wondering what was coming. More wine? A kiss? Something more bold?

He popped a strawberry into her mouth and after the dry wine the sweetness danced on her tongue. He dipped the fruit in champagne and painted her, her lips, her neck, easing the fabric of her nightdress lower on each pass until she was panting with need.

She expected to feel the cold wine applied by fruit on her nipples and was so shocked when she felt an entirely different sensation that she moaned. Her desire-fogged brain took a moment to process the fact that he'd stroked her with the rose petals.

"You are so beautiful," he murmured, making her feel as if she was both beautiful and special. Her heart was pounding, her desire moving from simmer to boil when he painted her nipples with wine-drenched berries. The cold and wet had her gasping and she could imagine that her nipples were standing on end with the combination of cold and excitement.

"I see goose bumps. You must be cold." Then he warmed the sensitive tips with his mouth.

She might be sightless, but she wasn't helpless. By reaching around she found the dish with the strawberries and, choosing one, reached toward him, feeding him the fruit, wondering what it would taste like warmed from his body, determined to find out.

When he planted a berry in her belly button she wasn't all that surprised. When he poured champagne over the top she gasped. "I missed dessert," he said, and then sucked the berry and the champagne from her navel.

Her hips were gyrating in wordless need and suddenly his mouth was there, feeding on her. After the slow teasing, she was so shocked to find him giving her everything she wanted that she couldn't hold herself back. With a cry she couldn't suppress, she let herself go, bursting on his tongue like one of his foolish strawberries.

He held her through the aftershocks, planting little kisses on her thighs, her belly, moving his way back up her body. "I wanted to make that last a whole lot longer," he said, in a low voice, "but I couldn't wait any longer."

"I'm glad."

She pulled off the blindfold, blinking in the light from the bedside lamp. Then she grinned at him. "I never got to the second part of my fantasy."

He swallowed, looking dubiously at the fabric swinging from her hand. "There's a part two?"

"Oh, yeah."

"You're sure you're not too tired?"

"Just getting started." Very deliberately, she set the dish of berries in easy reach.

"On your back, big guy."

17

KIRSTEN HAD NO IDEA WHAT TO DO or where to go. They'd had such a good time tonight, she and Sadhu. He made her feel like the woman she'd been briefly when she'd believed in herself and known she was capable of doing anything she strived to.

She liked that person, knew she could be her again if she put her mind to it. Especially if there was another person in the world who believed in her.

And then he'd done it again. After a wonderful evening when he'd made her laugh, made her feel like the most important woman in the world, when the brush of his fingers against her knee while they sat beside each other made her woozy with desire, he'd dropped her off at her place.

With a kiss on the cheek.

A kiss on the cheek!

That was the biggest insult of all.

She'd gone into her little rental house and flipped on the TV, but she couldn't concentrate.

Her last cigarette. She needed her last cigarette. The notion of dragging the smoke deeply into her lungs, the slight punch of light-headedness, the soothing calm that overtook her.

The white cylinder was in her bag. She ran for it, rummaged through to the bottom where it had fallen.

It had been crushed by all the junk she'd thrown in there. Damn it, why hadn't she been more careful? She sifted through and pulled out the pieces, but there was nothing there to smoke. She dropped the crushed mess of tobacco, paper and filter into the trash.

Emily. Emily had the rest of the pack of smokes. She was holding them for her. She glanced at her watch. It wasn't that late. She jumped into her car and drove to the Elk Crossing Lodge. Ran into the place, up the stairs to room 318. Luckily, she saw nobody around but a room service waiter going down the corridor. Somebody was lucky. They were getting champagne and two glasses and a red rose.

She got a kiss on the cheek.

She banged on the door.

Nothing.

Banged again.

Still nothing.

Then the foolishness of what she was doing struck her with painful clarity. Jonah and Emily were probably making love right now, not exactly interested in answering the door to a nicotine addict.

She turned away slowly and walked back to her car. What was she doing, anyway? There were gas stations, convenience stores. She could buy another pack.

Except she hadn't really wanted Emily to give them to her. She thought what she really wanted was some advice. Well, there was nobody around to whine to, so maybe she needed to suck it up and figure some things out for herself.

As she drove home, she had to accept that she'd already smoked her last cigarette.

She wasn't going back to cigarettes any more than she was going back to guys who didn't deserve her. And if Sadhu didn't want her after all, then maybe she'd be absolutely fine on her own.

She pulled into her drive, so preoccupied she didn't notice the green SUV parked on the street. When she got out and headed for the front door, she saw him.

Sitting on her front step with a bunch of red roses. Not one, but what looked like a couple dozen.

"Hi," she said.

"I wanted to stay away, but I couldn't."

"That is very good news."

She walked closer. He seemed nervous. He'd always been so confident around her, it was funny. He held out the flowers. "These are for you."

When was the last time a man had bought her flowers? So long ago, she didn't even own a vase.

"Thank you."

She opened the door and invited him in.

For something to do, she found an empty spaghetti sauce jar and filled it with water, putting the roses in carefully.

"There's something I have to tell you," Sadhu said.

"What is it?" Here it comes, she thought. The real reason he's been such a gentleman. The girlfriend, wife, boyfriend, whatever.

He walked up behind her. "This," he said softly, and turning her around, kissed her. Not on the cheek. But full on the mouth.

He kissed her long, and deep and with so much

passion she felt more light-headed than if she'd smoked an entire pack of cigarettes.

She smiled up at him, loving the dark richness of his eyes fringed with the prettiest eyelashes she'd ever seen. "All right, then."

He held on to her shoulders. "And I want you to know that I am finished playing hard to get." He kissed her lips, teased her with his tongue. "I want you to take me to your bed."

She wrapped her arms around his neck, digging her fingers deep into his luxurious hair, running her hands down his athletic fireman's back.

She set her hands on his hips and looked up at him. The truth was bright and glorious. "I don't think I'm ready."

Sadhu didn't look all that surprised. "It's different this time, isn't it? For both of us."

"I think so."

"Maybe I could stay for a while and we could watch a movie, or listen to music, or we could just talk."

"I think that would be wonderful."

EMILY PULLED HER EYELIDS open with an effort. It felt as though giant elephants were standing on them. She groaned as the perky announcer on the radio/alarm told her what a gorgeous day it was going to be in Elk Crossing.

Jonah had suggested they sleep the whole night in the other room, but naturally she hadn't taken her toothbrush with her and besides, this crazy room with the curtain and leaking roof had become special to her. It was theirs.

"And here's a shout-out to Leanne and Derek on their

special day. Lovebirds, this song is for you." And Percy Sledge's "When a Man Loves a Woman" boomed out.

Beside her, Jonah shifted. "Derek and Leanne's wedding is on the news?"

"Welcome to Elk Crossing."

He yawned hugely, reaching for her and burying his face in her neck, scratching her with his overabundant beard growth. The man was a walking testosterone pill.

She batted his hand away from her breast, though reluctantly. "I am supposed to be rested for the big day. Not sleep deprived." She rubbed at her eyes. "This is all your fault." But it was hard to inject any heat in her words, especially when the satisfied kitten-that-fell-into-the-cream-jug smile wouldn't leave her face.

"What?" he asked. "I gave you plenty of R & R, baby. Not much rest, perhaps, but plenty of relaxation."

Of course, she'd given him as much relaxation right back. As she forced herself to roll out of bed she consoled herself. She might have to spend an entire day in the world's ugliest dress, but at least she didn't have to play hockey. The most physically demanding task she'd be called on to perform was holding up Leanne's train. And she wasn't entirely sure she had the strength.

"What's the big rush?" he asked her, watching as she packed up her things. He had his head comfortably resting on his stacked hands, his elbows winged to the side so he looked like a dark, unshaven angel. "They aren't getting married until the afternoon."

She ticked off the tasks yet to be completed before the actual ceremony. "Hair. Makeup. Bride control." Her cell phone chirped letting her know she had a new text message. She checked who it was from and added another item to her list. "Kirsten control." She'd forgotten all about her confused friend's late-night visit to her room last night. She hoped whatever it was, Kirsten had figured things out.

"Let's see, we all get dressed at the bride's parents' house, then there are the before-the-ceremony pictures, then we'll all have a bit of a boo-hoo, which means makeup repair. Then the church."

"Sorry I can't make the ceremony. But I'll be there sometime tonight, as soon as the last game ends."

"Don't worry about it. I'll save you a dance."

When she had her bags ready, she ran into the bathroom to shower and brush her teeth. When she emerged, to her surprise, Jonah was up and in jeans and a T-shirt. "I'll help you put this stuff in your car."

"You don't have to," she said, feeling absurdly touched.

"Are you kidding? That dress alone will take three strong men to carry."

She looked at the thing with acute distaste now that the day when she would be forced to wear the thing had actually arrived. "I really love Leanne, but the woman has no taste in clothes."

"You don't have to tell me that." He hefted the huge dress off the closet door, turning this way and that. The skirt was so full it looked as though a headless, and surprisingly tasteless, Scarlett was dancing with an unshaven blue-jeaned Rhett.

Over the top of the orange satin his gaze met hers. "You know, I have this fantasy I haven't told you about yet."

"Really? It's quite a week for fantasies." When he looked at her his eyes darkened and she became suddenly breathless. She knew he was thinking about last night the way she was. She'd had some earthshaking sex in her life, but she didn't think anything could compare to what had happened between her and Jonah last night.

It wasn't only the way they'd played with each other's bodies and minds, it was the way they'd met on some deeper level than anything she'd ever experienced.

Tonight would be their last night together. Tomorrow Jonah had some kind of awards ceremony and brunch, and then he'd be heading back to Portland.

She had the present opening and a last lunch before Leanne and Derek took off on their honeymoon to Hawaii. And she returned to Portland.

Jonah hadn't said anything about getting together once they got back and she wasn't going to bring up the subject. It was strange, this had been such a bizarre affair from the very beginning. Two people who could credit bedbugs as their matchmakers couldn't have much of a future.

Could they?

The affair had happened with no thought, and she suspected both of them had entered into it because they were overcome with lust after sharing such close quarters. She didn't think they'd imagined anything more serious than a fling that was hot, fun, short and with no recriminations or painful goodbyes at the end.

But that was before last night.

Now, she had the uncomfortable feeling that once they left this room she'd be hit with the fact that it was more than a crazy fun holiday fling. That she was tied by some serious emotional strings to this man who could be so tough and yet so tender.

"Do you have time for breakfast before you go? We could get something in the coffee shop."

She shook her head. "No time."

"You have to eat. Breakfast is the most important meal of the day. Hang on a second." He danced the dress to his side of the room and dug through his duffel. Came out with a slightly dented, foil-wrapped bar, which he presented to her.

"This is a PowerBar snack." She read the label. "For recovery after strenuous exercise."

"You've had plenty of strenuous exercise in the past few hours. And it's better than going through the day with an empty stomach."

It was the first gift he'd ever given her. Not counting her fantasy, which she supposed was also a gift. Though perhaps more self-serving. It was a stupid meal replacement bar that had probably been in the bottom of his bag, forgotten, for weeks, but the idea that he cared enough to make sure she ate gave her a warm, goopy feeling inside that was like a danger flare suggesting there was nothing but emotional trouble ahead.

"Thanks," she said as casually as she could.

Pinning a bright smile on her face, she turned resolutely away and dragged her bag of essential wedding day stuff while Jonah hauled down the bridesmaid dress.

He pushed and shoved Big Orange into the backseat of her car. "If this dress was a person you'd need one of those extra long seat belts just to strap her in place."

"You know, maybe you shouldn't come tonight," she suddenly said, wondering where the words had come from. "I don't want your last memory of me to be of me wearing that dress."

He sent her an odd look but his tone was light when he said, "Don't worry. I fully intend that my last memory of you will be naked."

Then he kissed her and as she kissed him back she threw her arms around him. She might have even clung, just a little bit.

When they broke away she got into her car and started the engine. He waved and walked back toward the lodge.

Before pulling out she remembered Kirsten had left her a message. Probably she needed a ride.

The message read,

Can you fall in love in two days?

She stabbed at the buttons on her cell as she made her reply.

NO!

She kicked up gravel as she drove out of the parking lot, more aggressively than she'd intended.

No. No. NO!

Kirsten wasn't in love with Sadhu. The idea was ridiculous. She barely knew the guy. So, he'd played a different game than the one she was used to. The one most women were used to. Instead of trying relentlessly to get her into bed, he'd gone the opposite route. Teasing her with all his gorgeous exotic good looks and then making her work to get him into bed.

It was laughable how easily his little power play had worked.

Kirsten was experiencing an interesting variation on a game men and women had been playing since—well, since there were men and women. But love?

Love?

After two days?

That was as ridiculous as, say, Emily thinking she might have found love in less than a week.

Didn't happen.

The energy bar sitting on her passenger-side seat reflected the sunlight as she drove east, reminding her that she was hungry. She grabbed it off the seat, peeled open the paper and chomped into it.

Love in a few days. Good Lord. The idea was preposterous.

Anyway, love was just another power play. One that left the person doing the loving far too vulnerable.

She was going to have to have a woman-to-woman talk with Kirsten.

But first she had to detour to the florist and pick up all the bouquets for the wedding.

_18_

USUALLY, JONAH LOVED TO WIN. It was the whole point of playing hockey. Sure the camaraderie was nice, but he had his buddies and the guys on the force for that.

The exercise was definitely beneficial, but he was an athletic guy, he kept himself in shape. Which basically left winning as his main reason for loving hockey. Putting the puck in that sweet spot, watching it slide home past a colossus in padding, a helmet and the world's hugest gloves trying to stop it in its tracks. The moment he knew the puck was in and the winning goal had been scored, well, only nights like last night came close.

Tonight, however, he really wanted to lose. They'd played the semifinals this afternoon and tonight was the big game. The final. The one they'd been working toward all week.

All the Paters were ecstatic when they won their semifinal round, a bit of a squeaker. But not Jonah. He had a strange tickle behind his breastbone that told him he should be with Emily at that wedding.

Of course, it was a ridiculous impulse born of too much sex and too little sleep. Still, he had an absurd drive to protect her. If he didn't stop her, she'd "good daughter" her way into washing all the dishes.

And that wasn't the way she deserved to be treated. If Emily wouldn't stand up for herself, maybe she needed a little help from someone who'd be only too happy to tell them to wash their own dishes, print their own place cards, and choose a lot less dress to gown one of the prettiest bridesmaids he'd ever known. And he'd known quite a few.

But there were certain benefits to that dress. He hadn't been entirely facetious when he'd told her this morning that he had a fantasy revolving around that dress.

He pictured her standing in front of a long mirror, her hair up, that huge dress billowing out around her like an orange tent. And what did a guy do with a tent but crawl inside? Though he thought he'd prefer to watch her in the mirror while he lifted that skirt from the back. He suspected he could bare her backside and her long, dancer's legs while the front of her would look unmussed.

Yep, he didn't think he was going to be in any hurry to get that dress off her. But he was in a hurry to join her at the wedding.

He must be more sleep deprived than he'd realized because normally that itch behind his breastbone was his instinct about danger. But what danger could a woman be in during a family wedding? Unless that dress decided to take flight.

So he went back to playing. But whether it was because he wasn't fully focusing or because they were all getting tired, the Paters made a couple of dumb mistakes. And they were up against the best team in the tourney: the Alamo Ancients.

They were trailing by two when the first period

ended and if they didn't pull their act together, their title and the trophy were in jeopardy. *Focus,* Jonah ordered himself. He gave the guys a little pep talk, ending with, "All the free beer you can drink tonight to the next guy who scores."

As they were ready to hit the ice, his cell phone rang.

He went to get it but Kevin Lus grabbed his arm and hauled him toward the rink. "Come on, old man, your hottie can wait. Keep your focus and let's go win us a trophy."

Team spirit was at its peak so he joined in the rah-rah stuff and as he hit the ice, tried to concentrate on nothing but the art of hockey. Knowing where the players were, who was open, where the weakness in the Ancients' defense was, taking split-second advantage.

Sadhu got a break early in the second period. He powered past a defender, faked out the goalie and sent the puck flying home.

Now they were one down. And the best part was that Sadhu didn't drink beer, which had saved him a few bucks.

The crowd of spectators was as big as it ever got, which meant the rink was about half-full. A cheer went up. A pretty thin cheer. It would have been better if Emily and Kirsten were around.

They played doggedly on but they were all fatigued. His thigh was aching, sweat kept dripping in his eyes. The only consolation was that the other team was at least as tired as they were and tired players made mistakes.

Sure enough, the other team made one, their left wing losing attention exactly at the wrong moment. Kevin scooped the puck and, in a play they'd practiced countless times, Jonah powered forward toward the goal, taking Kevin's pass and sending it hurtling to the goal.

The goalie made a valiant effort, throwing himself onto the ice in front of the net, but he was a millisecond too late and the puck thumped home.

End of second period and the score was tied. Adrenaline was flowing and they were as pumped as kids.

He sucked back water and then remembered the phone call. He went for his cell. Listened to the message and instantly lost all interest in hockey. His whole body went cold and the itch that had nagged him clenched to a gripping pain.

"What are you doing?" Sadhu yelled at him as he was halfway through taking off his skates, his hands clumsy with haste.

"I gotta go."

"What?"

"Emily's in trouble."

"Say again?"

He didn't have time to explain. "Her cousin's a felon on the run. He's desperate, which makes him dangerous. I gotta go pick him up."

He finally got his skates off, jammed his feet into sneakers, grabbed his coat and bag and ran for the exit. He pounded to his truck. As he started the engine, he tried to call Emily on her cell phone but naturally the damn thing was turned off.

When the message beep came on he said, "Buddy's dangerous. Stay away from him. I'm on my way."

The passenger door of his truck swung open and Sadhu jumped in.

"What the hell are you doing?"

"Backup," he panted.

"You're a firefighter, not a cop."

"Shut up and drive."

He glanced in the rearview mirror as he backed out of his parking space and saw Portland Paters rushing out the door of the rink as if the place was on fire.

"What the hell?"

"They asked where you were going. I told them you had trouble you needed to take care of."

He didn't have time for this. He put his foot on the gas and roared out of the lot. Sadhu looked at the guys all running for vehicles and said, "You've got a lot of backup."

He stomped hard on the gas pedal wishing he had lights and a siren. Fortunately he knew where the Masonic Hall was, and he headed for it glad that this town was too small for traffic snarls.

"Look, you need to keep those guys away. I don't want the perp spooked."

"Maybe you'd better tell me what's going on."

Jonah sent him a quick glance, all he could spare from the road he was speeding down, and saw that the normally every-time-is-a-good-time Sadhu was looking steely eyed and ready for battle.

As though he'd spoken, Sadhu replied, "I've got an interest at that wedding myself."

"Turns out Third Cousin Buddy, you know the weasely balding orthodontist with the expensive wardrobe? He's a fugitive."

"A dentist? What did he do? Steal gold fillings?"

"Tax fraud. He refused to deal with insurance at all and made his patients pay up front for their treatment, and he let the patients deal with getting their insurance to reimburse them for the allowable amount their insurance company would pay."

"Okay."

Jonah barely slowed as he approached a four-way stop and, seeing nothing, gunned it through. "But he was only reporting one out of every three ortho cases to the IRS. The guy who called me says the average cost for each ortho case today is around six thousand and the average orthodontist has around three thousand active patients. You do the math."

Sadhu gave a low whistle. "He's billing close to two million a year. If he reports a third of his income, he's got well over a million a year cash going in his pocket."

"Or more likely into an offshore account somewhere. He's been at this racket for almost a decade."

But Sadhu was nobody's fool. "You look pretty intense for a guy chasing an embezzler."

"The IRS was tipped off by his nurse and longtime girlfriend. Lovers' quarrel? Guilty conscience? Who knows. She blew the whistle and agreed to testify since she was the one who looked after the paperwork and she knew all about the scam."

"Yeah?"

"Right before they were ready to arrest him, both Buddy and the nurse disappeared. The Feds figured they were on the run together and had made up their tiff."

The truck's tires squealed as he took a sharp corner. The last part made his hands tighten on the wheel and his foot push down harder. "They found the nurse last night. When they emptied the Dumpster behind her apartment."

"He killed his girlfriend? Shit."

"Yeah." Most white collar criminals were greedy but not violent. Buddy was now in a much more dangerous category.

Sadhu frowned. "Wait a minute, this guy steals millions. He murders a woman, goes on the lam and then comes to a family wedding? Makes no sense."

"It makes perfect sense. He's smart enough to know every border, airport, train and road will be watched. Cops all over the country have his picture. He uses a credit card or tries to rent a car and we've got him. So he comes to a third cousin's wedding, stays with relatives, eats his food at potlucks. Who's going to look for a dangerous fugitive at the Masonic Hall in Elk Crossing?"

"But the wedding's tonight. Then where's he going?"

"That's what's got me worried." They hit a pothole and the truck skewed to the right, skidding. He brought it back. "He's close to the Canadian border, but he's still got to get across it."

"How—"

"Shit!" He banged his fist against the wheel as the obvious answer hit him. "The message."

"What message?"

"Emily picked up Buddy's phone the night of the stagette thinking it was hers. Saw a message that said, 'Pickup, Saturday, midnight.'"

"Then we're in plenty of time." Sadhu glanced at the clock on the dash. "It's only nine-twenty."

"Who knows where this pickup is? I can't stand thinking of Emily in the same room with that monster."

"Or Kirsten," Sadhu said quietly.

They barreled through a red light, causing a blue Ford Taurus to screech its brakes and lay on the horn.

Sadhu said, "You got your wedding clothes with you? 'Cause you're going to blend in more easily if you change out of your hockey uniform."

"Clothes are at the hotel. No time."

"You have a plan?"

"Get that son of a bitch out of there and turn him over to the Feds."

"You think you should call the local cops in?"

"Don't want to spook the guy. We know he's capable of murder. Once I've got him away from the crowd, then I'll call the local cops."

He overtook and passed a car full of teenagers; they honked as he passed and tried to keep up, but fell behind after a block. The Masonic Hall came into view and reluctantly Jonah slowed the truck.

"How'd he kill her? The nurse?"

"Bullet in the back of the head."

Jonah saw Sadhu's hands clench. Knew the feeling. "You got a gun with you?"

"Never carry a weapon when I'm not on duty."

"You sure you don't want me to go in with you?"

"No. He's expecting me to be there. Two of us show up? Might freak him out."

"Watch yourself."

"Yeah." He parked then slid out of the truck, aches and pains gone as the adrenaline carried him forward to do his job. To protect his woman. Before slamming the truck door he leaned in to Sadhu. "You're clear?"

"Yeah. Keep the rest of the team out here, call the cops once you've got Cousin Buddy outside and away from the crowd."

He nodded. "If I'm not outside in five minutes, call the cops anyway."

"You got it."

A nod and he headed toward the entrance. He heard dance music as he got closer, a good sign. And when he opened the door, the scene was as placid as an old folks' home on a Sunday afternoon. A few couples dancing, some groups settled around tables, talking. He scanned the entire room in one thorough sweep.

Two huge orange dresses—one belonged to a blonde who was a lot shorter than Emily. He spied the second on the dance floor. The woman was a brunette, with her back to him, and she was dancing with Third Cousin Buddy.

He felt the hair stand up on the back of his neck as he strode forward, nothing clear in his mind but the need to get that animal off her. Now.

Buddy saw him and stopped dead, his eyes widening, panic and the sure knowledge that he'd been found out flashed on his face like a series of neon signs.

All Jonah cared about was Emily. Separate her from the murdering orthodontist, then he'd deal with Buddy. As he drew closer he forced a smile to his fury-stiff lips. "Emily, I came as soon as I could get away. Didn't even stop to change clothes."

He was four feet from Cousin Buddy, three feet. Buddy shoved his dance partner at Jonah and then turned and sprinted for a door.

The woman turned, gasping. "What the hell?"

The world went cold and still for a second. She wasn't Emily. He grabbed her arm. "Where's Emily?"

"Ow." She pulled her arm away. "How should I know?"

He glanced around, shouted, "Where's Emily?"

Emily's mother rose, acting like a society hostess with a difficult guest. "Hello, Jonah. So nice you could make it. And in your hockey uniform."

"Where is she?" His urgency must have got through.

"In the kitchen, dear. She won't be long." She gestured to the door Cousin Buddy had disappeared behind.

Jonah sprinted after him, his need to get Emily safe the force that drove him forward. He'd break Buddy's neck with his bare hands if he touched her and the thieving, lying, murdering dentist better know it.

He bashed through the door before it had finished swinging.

19

"A HUNDRED AND THREE, and another dozen makes… um…a hundred-fifteen." And next time she was definitely going to say no to picking up the rental dishes which, like so many seemingly simple tasks, was a lot more complicated. Here she was checking that all the dishes were accounted for against the rental agreement. Since she'd signed for the dishes yesterday when she picked them up and she was pretty sure she'd be returning them tomorrow, she was determined to keep track.

"Emily, I need your help," Cousin Buddy said, coming in behind her in a big rush.

"Get in line."

"Come on." He grabbed her arm. "I'm too drunk to drive and I promised Derek I'd pick something up for him."

He was breathing heavily as if he'd been running, and he pulled her arm so hard she dropped the clipboard.

"Ask somebody else. I've got to—"

The door banged open a second time and then everything happened so fast she couldn't keep track. Jonah was standing there looking a little like a superhero in his padded red uniform. He'd obviously rushed all the way over here without bothering to change, but he didn't seem happy to see her. In fact, he wasn't looking at her but at Buddy, who was behind her, outside her line of vision, still gripping her arm.

"Buddy, I'd like to talk to you outside."

"I don't think so," her cousin said with a chilling lack of intonation that for some reason made her flesh creep. She turned her head to look at him and as she did so she noticed he had one of the carving knives from the baron of beef that had been served at the wedding dinner. He held it as though he were about to carve a roast, or perform surgery on one of his patients.

She made an instinctive move away from him, toward Jonah, but before she'd taken a step Cousin Buddy tightened his grip and toppled her hard against him and held the knife to her throat.

It was like something out of a bad movie, not the kind of thing that happens to a person at their cousin's wedding. She wanted to believe this unpleasant charade was some kind of bad practical joke, but Jonah was pale and rigid with control, every inch the cop. And she could smell Buddy's sweat, and something else, a smell she thought was fear.

"What's going on?" she managed to say, even though her throat was dry and the knife was pressing her neck in a way that cut across her jugular. She could feel her pulse bumping against the cool, slightly greasy steel. Of course, an orthodontist must have studied basic anatomy. He hadn't found her jugular by accident.

What was going on she had no idea, but it was obvious she had to find a way out of the mess, preferably before any of her blood was spilled.

"Emily? Jonah? Is everything all right?" her mother called through the door.

"Keep her out," Buddy said, pressing the knife so she had to press her lips together to keep from crying out.

A sharp wave of protectiveness for her mother swamped her. Whatever happened, she couldn't let her mother see this. "Everything's fine, Mom," she called out, amazed at how normal she sounded.

Her mom giggled. "I think they're making out. He sure was in a hurry to see her."

"Throw me your keys," Buddy snapped at Jonah.

And she realized the truck keys were still hanging in his hand.

"Throw them to my left, over her head. And don't do anything stupid that would get Emily hurt."

"Look," Jonah said, "I'll drive you wherever you want. Let Emily go."

"I'm not taking your truck. Or you. Throw me the keys."

He tossed them and Buddy caught them neatly. "Now. My cousin and I are going for a little drive. If you follow, I'll kill her. If you don't, I'll let her go. As simple as that."

And he began to pull her toward the kitchen door that led to the back parking lot.

Jonah didn't move. But he didn't stay quiet, either. "You think I'm the only cop who knows where you are? You'll be picked up before you've gone a block. Drop the knife, let Emily go and I'll help you make a deal."

"Nobody's going to follow me or she dies. That's the deal we're making." Buddy opened the kitchen door and stepped out, pulling her with him.

Out of her peripheral vision she saw the flash of a familiar red uniform and hope flared, but Buddy only pulled her closer to his body. "Don't even think about it," he snarled.

As he pulled her backward, her high heels and the damn fool dress making her stumble over the cracked pavement, she saw Sadhu, looking more grim than she'd believed possible. And standing with him, the entire team of Portland Paters as well as a few guys in a green uniform she didn't recognize.

Jonah emerged from the kitchen door after them, but then stood, a statue of anguished fury.

Their gazes connected and all doubts she'd harbored that a person could fall in love in a few days were gone. Who ever knew how many days they had in a given life? That she should have wasted a second of her time with Jonah made her crazy angry. She hadn't even known she loved him until today, so she hadn't had a chance to tell him.

She told him now, though, with her eyes. Opened herself up and let him see everything in her heart.

Damn it, she wasn't ready to die. Or to let Buddy maul her in this humiliating way.

Buddy pulled her to an older-model car, a big boat of a thing that had to be thirty years old. If there was a chance, it would be now. He'd have to let her go to open the car door. If she could pull away, just a foot or two, she knew that would give Jonah all the opening he needed.

She heard a jingle of keys. Braced herself.

Get ready to run, Jonah's eyes telegraphed to her. His body was coiled energy, waiting, ready.

I'm ready, she let him know. All Buddy had to do

was lessen the pressure and she'd duck and roll. She might end up hurt, but he couldn't do anything serious before an entire hockey team of seriously pissed off guys was on him.

"Open the door," he said, holding the knife steady against the most vulnerable part of her throat. He hadn't locked the car. And she knew that he wasn't going to give her the chance she needed.

She fumbled, and he pressed the knife harder. She opened the passenger-side door.

He pushed her in and stayed right with her, pushing her hip along the bench seat until she was behind the wheel. "You drive."

She heard a click and pop and then the knife's pressure lessened. She turned her head and found that her danger hadn't decreased at all. He'd popped open the glove compartment and pulled out a mean-looking handgun.

Once she'd driven them out of the parking lot, he directed her. "Turn left, then right at the intersection."

"You're not going to kill me." She tried to infuse her tone with absolute certainty. "We're cousins. Family doesn't kill family."

"I don't want to hurt you, Emily, but I will do whatever I have to do to get out of here."

Her head was starting to ache. "I don't understand."

"Let me make it very simple for you. I've got more money than you've ever dreamed of in a few accounts in parts of the world where they aren't too fussy about where your money came from so long as you've got lots of it. It's time for me to go join up with my cash and spend the rest of my life trying to spend it." His smugness was appalling.

"But what about your practice?"

"I'm taking early retirement." He chuckled, a truly unpleasant sound. "Freedom forty. I like the sound of that."

"How are you going to get there?"

He skewed his head to look behind them, something he'd been doing a lot of. "Drive faster."

"I'm too nervous. I'll crash." He must see that she wasn't bluffing. She could barely keep the unfamiliar car on the road as it was. It was a big boat of a thing that must be thirty years old with oversensitive power steering and poorly aligned wheels. "And this car's a piece of junk. If you're so rich, can't you afford something better?"

He rose to the bait as she'd suspected he would. If there was one thing she knew about Buddy it was that he loved his luxury goods and flaunted his large income in every way possible. "I bought it for cash because it's inconspicuous. I'll dump it when I leave. Don't you worry. From now on I'll be in chauffeured limos."

He sent her a crafty glance. "Why don't you come with me? I've got plenty of money for two. I'm a way better catch than that cop you're so hot for. His net worth is probably in his hockey equipment."

What turnip truck did he think she'd fallen off? He was as likely to take her to his banking paradise as Jonah was to sit in that parking lot and wait for the phone call saying he could come pick her up.

"HE HAS A GUN," SADHU said grimly.

"I saw it."

As the old Cutlass pulled out of the lot, a grim-faced Emily at the wheel, Jonah had never felt so helpless or so frightened. He didn't like either feeling. He was a man of action and he knew that his personal feelings for Emily were getting in the way of logical thought, paralyzing him. He had to get his personal fear for her safety out of the way or he'd jeopardize his ability to save her.

There were a few seconds of tense silence. "We have to go after them," Kevin Lus suddenly said as though he couldn't stay quiet.

"He said he'd kill her if we followed," Jonah said.

The kitchen door opened once more and Kirsten ran out, looking puzzled. "What are you all doing out here?"

Sadhu crossed the gravel in two strides and pulled her into his arms. He hugged her so hard she squeaked in protest and pulled back slightly, obviously sensing the trouble in his face. "What's happened? What is it?"

She glanced around, and saw Jonah. "Where's Emily?"

A look passed between Sadhu and Jonah. He walked over. "I don't have time to explain the details but Buddy's got Emily. He's kidnapped her."

"What?"

"He's a criminal, Kirsten. He's holding a gun on her."

The soft brown eyes opened wide. "Why?"

"He needs to escape. My best guess is he's trying to get to Canada."

"It would take about three hours to drive to the closest border crossing. They'd take State Highway 1, but I don't think the crossing's open again until morning."

Jonah shook his head. "He can't risk a border crossing. He needs to sneak into Canada. He got a text message Thursday confirming pickup at midnight Saturday. Who's picking him up and how? I'm guessing a small plane. Where's the airport from here?"

"The airport's forty minutes away, but even a private plane has to log its flight plan."

"How about a private airport?"

She shook her head. Her forehead was creased with worry. "I don't know. Derek's uncle Tim is at the wedding. He comes into our restaurant and I've talked to him a few times. He's taken some hunting trips to Canada. He might know."

"We've got to bring in the cops. Maybe the Feds?" Sadhu said. "They've got the resources and equipment."

"But they'll put the emphasis on catching Buddy. My priority is Emily."

"Agreed."

One thing he was certain of was that he couldn't sit here doing nothing. "Kirsten, you said Derek's uncle is a hunter?"

She nodded.

"Where does he keep his guns?"

"At home, I think. Locked up."

"Close to here?"

"I don't know where he lives."

"Okay. Go get him. Bring him out quietly. But hurry." He glanced at his watch. "We've got two hours until midnight."

He didn't say what he was thinking. He had two hours to get Emily back alive.

20

DEREK'S UNCLE TIM, WAS A burly, grizzled millwright in his early sixties. He didn't waste any time but as soon as he'd grasped the situation took them straight to his house, which was less than five minutes' drive. He pulled out his three hunting rifles, binoculars and a comprehensive map of the northern part of the state.

"He won't use public airstrips. But there are private strips here—" he jabbed a work-gnarled finger at the map "—here and here."

He studied the map another minute. "A helicopter could land in a field just about anywhere, and then there are the floatplanes."

Jonah looked at him. From the second he'd heard about the situation he'd been calm and focused. And he approached the problem as though it was a battle plan. "You ever in the military?"

"Army. Served in Vietnam."

"If you were trying to get out of here quietly tonight, how would you go?"

He studied the map for a minute. "Easiest and safest would be a floatplane from the lake. Fly straight into B.C. and land on another lake or river, maybe even get to the coast."

"How many ways into the lake?"

"The main road, which Buddy'll have to take, driving that big Cutlass. But there are some secondary routes I can take in my 4x4."

"Okay." He split the remaining volunteers into teams of two and assigned each team one of the locations Tim had identified as a possible escape spot. "Nobody approaches the vehicle. If you see the Olds, or hear or see a plane approaching, immediately call me or Sadhu on our cell phones. Everybody clear on that? This guy's armed and dangerous and he has a hostage. Do not approach."

"Got it, Jonah."

"Tim, we'll take the lake. Sadhu and I'll come with you." And they took the three rifles.

He'd barely noticed that Kirsten was still with him until she spoke. "Tim, do you have any sweats or anything that Emily could change into? It's cold out there and she has nothing on but that dress." She hesitated. "Also, if you have a first aid kit?"

"Good points. Thanks, Kirsten." He'd thought of her as nothing but a party girl; he was pleased to find her levelheaded and competent in an emergency.

"My son's room is the third door on the left. He's eighteen. Help yourself to anything he's got. I've got a first aid kit in the truck."

"Thanks."

She was back in less than two minutes. She'd changed into jeans and a dark sweatshirt, she had a set of sweats in her hand. "I'm coming with you."

"But—"

"Emily's my friend and she might need me."

"It could be dangerous," Jonah protested.

"Bite me," she said and climbed into the back of Tim's 4x4.

IT WAS HARD TO THINK WHEN your third cousin was pointing a gun at you and forcing you to drive down a country road in a too-big car you'd never driven before while wearing a too-big dress, too-high heels and too-big hair.

But Emily was doing her best.

What she'd begun to understand was that Buddy was a lot more dangerous than she'd believed. And that he was really enjoying having her at his mercy. There was an odd expression in his eyes that truly creeped her out. He seemed more than usually smug, as if he had a big treat to look forward to.

She was no psychiatrist but she thought he genuinely wanted her to be frightened, was becoming aroused by her helplessness. This infuriated her, but she also thought it might give her some leverage when she needed it. So she acted more scared than she was. She even let him believe she might be thinking of going with him.

As if.

He might be enjoying toying with her, but her apparent willingness to go along with him, and her attempts to let him see her fear weren't making him do anything convenient like put that damn gun away. She'd seen him stash the knife under the floor mat on his side of the car so he could reach it quickly, and she couldn't.

They'd been driving beside the lake for a while now. The only, lonely car on the road. None of the cabins showed light. Maybe it was too late in the season. The streetlights were few and far between.

Once she stamped her foot on the brake and instead of throwing the gun from his hand, her action made him jam the gun into the side of her breast. "Do that again and I shoot."

She had no doubt he was telling the truth.

"Something ran across the road," she said, making her voice quake. "I didn't want to hit it."

"Don't stop again until I tell you to."

She tried to cry, but she was too angry to fake tears. He was nothing but an overgrown bully, worse for the fact that he must have been a geeky weakling as a kid. Now he was a what? Sociopath, she supposed, thinking he could take whatever he wanted regardless of society's rules.

She became aware of a second engine, and glancing up saw lights approaching from the air. A floatplane headed for the lake.

Buddy noticed, too, and his self-satisfied air grew intolerable. "Excellent. Right on time." He glanced at her. "Pull up at the public dock."

She did as she was told, the car wheels kicking up gravel as she turned in to the empty lot.

It was cold and her bridesmaid dress wasn't keeping her very warm.

"Get out," Buddy said. "And you can stop shivering. I'm not going to kill you here. You're coming with me. When we get to Canada, we'll see." He ran his gaze over her body. "If you make yourself useful enough, I might take you with me after all." He ran his finger down her throat, settling his hand over her breast. "But you'll have to work at it. I'm very demanding."

She wrenched the door open and got out. She tried to take the keys with her, but with a chiding laugh he grabbed them away from her.

The plane dropped and landed smoothly in the middle of the lake. Buddy got out leisurely. He didn't seem worried that she'd run and, really, where would she go? They were in the middle of nowhere. If she tried to run, in these heels, he'd simply shoot her.

He went round to the trunk of the car and popped it open, retrieving a bag. Inside was a large flashlight. He flicked on the strong beam and held it up, then collected Emily and urged her toward the dock.

Her heels were treacherous on the gravel and it was dark so she could barely see anything. The wind was whipping up off the lake and she knew her skin was covered in goose bumps.

"Are there any clothes in that bag? I'm freezing. I'd really like to change out of this dress before I get on a plane."

He sighed. "Emily, be a good girl and come with me quietly."

And just like that, something in Emily snapped. All these years she'd been the good girl. The reliable one. If there was a family chore, call Emily.

She'd picked up cakes and china and bouquets, she'd dressed in an orange tent and worn these terrible curls without complaint, but being dragged along as a hostage was it. The proverbial straw.

They were halfway up the dock by this time and the floatplane was almost alongside the upper edge.

"No," she said calmly. "No. I won't. I'm sick of being a good girl."

He was already juggling his bag, the flashlight and

the gun. She stumbled into him, and as he turned to her, trying to get control, she stamped her ridiculous high heel into his instep with all the force of her pent-up anger.

He grunted with the pain and dropped the bag, but not the gun.

Before he could steady the gun on her, she yelled, "And I'm not going anywhere with you," and while he was off balance, she shoved him off the dock.

The flashlight wheeled in a crazy circle as it fell from his hand. The gun discharged, an explosion in her ear, and then Buddy was falling off the dock.

As his empty hands scrabbled to save himself, they grabbed the fabric of her huge skirt.

"No." She kicked at his hands, but he hung on grimly and when he went over the side, she and the dress went with him.

The water was cold. So cold it took her breath away.

The plane, which had slowed almost to a stop beside the dock, didn't cut its engine.

Buddy yelled and started to swim toward it.

All she wanted was to get to the dock and climb up onto dry land. Buddy could fly as far away as he pleased so long as he didn't take her with him.

She heard the roar of the plane's engine increase and vaguely realized it was spinning away from them, and she watched it turn and glide away from her. Buddy's shouts grew frantic, but the plane kept going, taking off in the night like an impossibly large sea bird.

She tried to swim for the dock but her dress hampered her. She managed to kick off her shoes, but when she tried to move forward the dress acted like an anchor, pulling her back. And down.

She heard another engine, saw lights coming crazily toward her. She wanted to call out, but she was so cold, and the waterlogged fabric was getting heavy.

She fought the pull of the dark lake, but she was tiring.

Jonah's voice sounded. "Emily!"

He yelled for her, over and over. "I'm here," she managed to shout once, weakly.

Stomping feet. "Damn it, it's too dark. Emily, where are you?"

"Here," she said, her voice but a whisper. Her legs were trying to hold her up but the water was over her chin.

"Hold on, I'm coming."

She heard a splash. Not very near her, but it was nice of him to come looking for her. She tried to move toward where she'd heard the splash, but she didn't think she'd moved at all. She tasted lake water and coughed.

A light. The flashlight. Somebody had found the flashlight.

She watched the beam bob over the surface, then blinked when it struck her. "There she is." It was Kirsten's voice. "Look, the orange dress."

"Hi, Kirsten," she said, but when she opened her mouth more lake water flowed in and she coughed again, this time going under.

She heard splashing and suddenly strong arms were pulling her up. "Hang on, hang on, baby. I've got you."

"Jonah," she sighed, and hung on.

Kirsten kept the flashlight trained on them and when Jonah hoisted her up, Sadhu and Derek's uncle Tim hauled her up to the dock surface. She wondered what Tim was doing there but was too cold to ask.

She was so cold. Sadhu stripped off his team jersey and wrapped it around her, Tim yanked off his jacket.

Jonah appeared beside her, dripping and shivering. "You okay?"

"Yes." She managed around chattering teeth. He took her face in his hands and then kissed her, his lips almost as cold as hers, but she felt all the warmth behind them.

"Let's get you warm."

"Where's B-Buddy?" she asked.

"Bastard got away." He gestured angrily to the sky. "When I heard that shot, and then the plane took off…"

He gulped. "If I ever get my hands on that son of a bitch…"

She shook her head. "He's n-not on the p-plane. I pushed him off the d-dock. He's in the water somewhere."

She heard the sound of sirens. Two of them, which meant Elk Crossing had its full force of law on board. Two squad cars squealed to a halt and Jonah said, "Perfect timing, they can help us haul Buddy's sorry ass out of the water. I'd be too tempted to drown him."

"You're shivering your ass off," Kirsten told him tartly. "Take Emily and get in Tim's vehicle. I cranked the heat up. Emily, I brought you some fresh clothes. I had a feeling you might need them."

"You're an angel," she said but her teeth were chattering so hard she doubt anyone could have understood her. Jonah didn't let her totter to her feet, he scooped her up and carried her.

Of course, her fingers were too stiff to get out of the dress by herself, so Jonah helped her, peeling the wet silk from her clammy skin and dressing her swiftly in sweats that mysteriously said Elk Crossing High.

"You don't have any dry clothes," she said to him.

"That's okay. I wasn't in the water as long as you. I'll dry off on the way home."

They didn't talk after that, simply held each other while more vehicles arrived and an odd collection of aging hockey players, four police officers, Kirsten and Tim searched for Buddy. They found him.

He'd tried to swim for shore, but the cold had slowed him too much.

The last Emily saw of him, he was being escorted to the squad car. His glasses were missing as were his shoes, so he blinked owlishly and limped on the gravel. His skin was as pale and wet as raw tuna, his lips were blue and he shivered violently.

After he'd been taken away, a police officer came and knocked on the window and Jonah rolled it down. "I'm going to need statements from both of you."

"Tomorrow," Jonah said. The officer looked at the pair of them and nodded. "First thing in the morning."

Tim got into the driver's seat looking very pleased with the night's work. She had a feeling he'd be a local hero for some time to come. In a town like this where people worked hard their whole lives, went to church, paid their taxes and probably worked overtime to get their kids' teeth straightened, nobody would have any sympathy for a guy like Buddy who ripped off decent people. The fact that Tim wasn't related to Buddy would also help.

Sadhu and Kirsten grabbed a ride with Kevin Lus, so there were only the three of them. Jonah filled them both in on the background of Buddy, most of which Buddy had already told her. When he got to the part about the murdered nurse, she gasped. Jonah's arm tightened around her. She understood then how close she had come to dying tonight.

They asked to be dropped at the hotel. Tim met her eyes in the rearview mirror. "Your mom will be worried about you."

"Tell her I'm okay, will you? I need a hot shower and bed. It's been a crazy night. I'll see everyone at the present-opening brunch tomorrow."

He nodded. "I'll tell them."

Jonah gripped the man's hand as he got out. "Thanks. It was good working with you."

"Likewise."

Tim eyed the mound of wet orange bundled on the floor. "What do you want me to do with that dress?"

She shuddered.

Jonah said, "I've got it." He scooped the silk up and staggered across the lot with it in his arms. The dress looked like a half-deflated life raft. She had no idea what he was planning until he went around the side of the lodge to the industrial Dumpsters. She took great satisfaction in watching him stuff the last of Big Orange into the trash.

THE WATER STREAMED over her skin, hot and pumping steam. She absorbed the heat into her body any way she could, breathing the steam, letting it enter her open pores and be rubbed in by Jonah's gentle hands.

"This is not how I planned our first shower together would go," he said, their naked bodies resting gently against each other while the water warmed them both. His eyes were tender, the dark lashes spiked with water droplets.

She couldn't help herself, she reached up and kissed

his wet mouth. "I know. I figured our last night together would be wild, but not I-almost-got-murdered-by-a-killer-orthodontist-who-also-happens-to-be-my-third-cousin wild."

"I'll make it up to you when we get back to Portland," he promised her, turning her gently so he could soap her back.

"That's the first time you've ever said anything about seeing each other when we got back to Portland."

His hands stilled. "Are you kidding me? You think after a week with you I could ever let you go?"

She smiled at the white ceramic shower tiles. "Personally, no, I do not."

21

"OH, EM, I'M SO GLAD YOU'RE all right." Her mother rushed up to her and threw her arms around her. "I don't know what I'd do if anything ever happened to my little girl." Emily hugged her back tightly. That was the thing with family. They drove you crazy, but who else loved you like your mom?

They were in the front entrance hall of Leanne's parents' house where relatives and close friends had been invited for the present opening and a final brunch before the wedding was finally and officially over.

"I'm fine. Really." But she couldn't help teasing a little. "Good thing I didn't let you set me up with Cousin Buddy, though."

"Oh, don't even talk to me about that little shit," her mom said. Emily was so shocked her mouth fell open. Her mother had never used an expletive in her hearing. Never.

"You look beautiful, dear. Are you feeling all right? You should have gone to the hospital."

"I'm fine. A hot shower and a long sleep were all I needed."

She was wearing one of her own outfits today, a pale green two-piece with large buttons by a designer not carried in Wal-Mart. She'd left her hair hanging free.

Beside her, Jonah wore the slacks and blazer he'd brought for the hockey banquet he'd skipped so he could be with her. He kept her hand in his as much as possible and she let him, understanding some part of the fear he'd felt when he thought he'd lost her.

Maybe they'd been too tired and traumatized to do more than hold each other last night, but this morning when they'd woken, they'd made love with a sweetness and intensity that told her louder than any words that she was loved.

"Well, come on in and make yourselves comfortable. You're the last ones here, but I explained you'd be a little late because you had to give the police your statements."

The party was in full swing when they got into the living room, and after demanding her story, everyone let the focus shift back to Leanne and Derek.

Kirsten came out of the kitchen, followed by Sadhu, both bearing casserole dishes for the dining table. When Kirsten saw her she came over for a hug and Sadhu did the manly fist-touching thing with Jonah.

Kirsten was wearing the smoking-cessation patch; in typical Kirsten fashion, she'd chosen to stick the thing not in some inconspicuous place under her clothes, but on her chest like a tattoo or a piece of jewelry, as though daring anyone to comment.

As far as Emily could tell, no one had. Any more than they were taking issue with the fact that Tyler had been replaced on her arm with Sadhu. Altogether a much more appropriate choice.

It felt strange not to be bringing out the casseroles and fetching forgotten condiments, but she supposed that a near death experience was a good excuse for getting the day off. As she collected her plate from the stack at the brunch table, she started and left the line to find her mother. "Mom, I never returned the dishes to the rental place."

"Of course not. When Kirsten and Sadhu got back last night I asked them to take care of it for you. Kirsten's a lovely girl, she's so helpful. She reminds me of you that way." Her mom beamed at her. "Well, let's get some food."

After the gift opening, Emily found an excuse to haul Kirsten upstairs to Leanne's bedroom.

"So?"

Kirsten hugged her. "It's so amazing. I've never known anyone like Sadhu. He believes in me. I mean, he really does. And he doesn't let me play any of my usual games." She giggled. "At least, not outside the bedroom."

"So he finally, you know, put out?"

They both snorted with laughter and Kirsten said, "Oh, yeah. Last night when we got back to my place we couldn't hold off anymore. And, honey, it was so worth the wait."

"So are you guys going to do the long-distance thing?"

"No. I'm already pulling my résumé together. I need to get out of Elk Crossing and find a new job. I'm checking out lots of places, but as it turns out, one of the guys on the Paters works for a TV network and he's got the connections to get me an interview at least. The rest is up to me."

"That would be great if we lived in the same town." She grinned at her friend. "We could double-date. I'm keeping my fingers crossed."

But she knew whatever happened, Kirsten had herself back on the right path.

They talked for a few more minutes, filling each other in and commiserating on the events of the previous evening.

"I'm going down now," Kirsten said. "You wait a few minutes and follow me. I don't want the guys knowing we were yapping."

"Okay."

She spent a few minutes looking through the wedding photos that had already been uploaded onto Leanne's computer. She shook her head at the butt ugly bridesmaid dresses, but Leanne and Derek sure looked happy. All in all, it had been an eventful wedding, but a pretty good one.

She was about to leave the room again when she heard her mother's voice calling to Leanne's mother. There was a furtive quality to the low tone that made her stand still and listen.

"Yes, Margaret? What is it?" Leanne's mom answered. They were in the hallway so she could hear every word.

"It's about the Masonic Hall. I want to book it for next June. I know it books up fast. What was the name of the person you spoke to? And do you have their number handy?"

What on earth did her mother want with the Masonic Hall? Mostly the family only booked it for big occasions like ruby anniversaries and weddings.

"That's a wonderful idea. When I saw the two of them together I knew."

"Of course, nothing's official yet, so don't say anything, but the sooner I get on with the arrangements the sooner I can give my daughter the wedding of her dreams."

Puzzlement turned to horror. Her mother only had one daughter. And that was Emily. Who was not— repeat *not*—getting married in the Masonic Hall. Wedding of her dreams? Try nightmare from hell.

Besides, nobody had asked her to marry them.

Yet.

She'd only known Jonah for a few days. They hadn't even said "I love you" yet. Not in actual words, anyway.

She shook her head. Her mother was doing it again. Trying to manipulate her, control her life. Emily's dream wedding was eloping. No. Too complicated. City hall at noon. In a pair of jeans and carrying a bunch of daisies from a street vendor. Much better.

Then the rotating wedding photos on Leanne's computer screen caught her eye. Her family all together, celebrating.

For just one moment she allowed herself to imagine the bridesmaid dress she would force on every woman who'd ever made her don a bad bridesmaid gown. Her fertile imagination inventing truly hideous confections.

It was fun to imagine, but she needed to stop her mother before her crazy idea went any further.

She gave the two older women time to get back downstairs and then followed.

Jonah and Sadhu were high-fiving each other when she got down, Kirsten laughing in delight.

"What's going on?"

Sadhu answered. "Well, you know we forfeited the trophy when we didn't complete the championship game last night. Because Sir Galahad here had to ride off and rescue his woman."

"Yes. I'm sorry about that."

Jonah looked acutely uncomfortable at that view of things. "That's not what—"

"Give it up. So at the banquet, they announced a new category. The Portland Paters won the Most Sportsmanlike Team award."

"That's great."

"That's what I figured. A team is like a family. You stick together. Minute they learned Jonah was in trouble, you should have seen the guys come running out to help."

A shrill voice called out, "They're leaving. Derek and Leanne are leaving."

The just-married couple laughed and waved as they drove off in Uncle Bill's Cadillac with the Just Married sticker in the back window and empty cans rattling behind in the road.

Not long after, Emily was also ready to say her goodbyes. "Oh, do you have to go so soon?" her mom asked.

"I've got a long drive ahead of me."

Her mother hugged her long and hard. "Well, we'll see you soon. Dad and I are planning to come down to visit for a few days later in the spring." She turned to Jonah. "And it's been a real pleasure getting to know you, Jonah. I'm looking forward to seeing lots more of you."

"Mom."

Jonah pretended he hadn't heard her embarrassed interjection. "I'm looking forward to that, too, Mrs. Saunders."

"Oh, please, call me Margaret."

Emily's clothes were creased from all the hugging by the time she got out of there.

"So, I was thinking," he said as they drove together back to their hotel to check out and leave.

"Yes?"

"You know this fantasy of yours?"

Heat washed slowly over her body.

"Which fantasy would that be?"

He slid his hand over and wrapped his warm hand around her upper thigh. "The room service waiter?"

"Oh, that one."

"I was thinking how flexible it is."

"Flexible?"

"Sure. Every time the room service waiter lifts that silver thing—we're really going to have to figure out the proper name for it, by the way—there can be different things under there. I've already come up with quite a few ideas I'd like to try when we get home."

When we get home. She knew he meant Portland and yet there was something between them that was deep and special. Somehow she'd never found a minute to talk to her mom and stop her from booking Emily and Jonah's wedding next year at the Masonic Hall.

His hand was warm on her thigh, his profile was tough and sexy; he'd disrupted her life from the moment he stepped into it wearing boxer shorts and removing a bedbug from the hysterical woman. In six short days he'd driven her crazy, surprised her, shocked her, given her some of the best sex of her life and saved her from a homicidal maniac.

A lot could happen between now and next June. Besides, who else could she possibly marry?

* * * * *

*Celebrate 60 years of pure reading pleasure
with Harlequin®!
Just in time for the holidays,
Silhouette Special Edition® is proud to present*
New York Times *bestselling author
Kathleen Eagle's*
ONE COWBOY, ONE CHRISTMAS

Rodeo rider Zach Beaudry was a travelin' man—
until he broke down in middle-of-nowhere South
Dakota during a deep freeze. That's when an
angel came to his rescue....

"Don't die on me. Come on, Zel. You know how much I love you, girl. You're all I've got. Don't do this to me here. Not *now*."

But Zelda had quit on him, and Zach Beaudry had no one to blame but himself. He'd taken his sweet time hitting the road, and then miscalculated a shortcut. For all he knew he was a hundred miles from gas. But even if they were sitting next to a pump, the ten dollars he had in his pocket wouldn't get him out of South Dakota, which was not where he wanted to be right now. Not even his beloved pickup truck, Zelda, could get him much of anywhere on fumes. He was sitting out in the cold in the middle of nowhere. And getting colder.

He shifted the pickup into Neutral and pulled hard on the steering wheel, using the downhill slope to get her off the blacktop and into the roadside grass, where she shuddered to a standstill. He stroked the padded dash. "You'll be safe here."

But Zach would not. It was getting dark, and it was already too damn cold for his cowboy ass. Zach's battered body was a barometer, and he was feeling South Dakota, big time. He'd have given his right arm to be climbing into a hotel hot tub instead of a brutal blast of north wind. The right was his free arm anyway.

Damn thing had lost altitude, touched some part of the bull and caused him a scoreless ride last time out.

It wasn't scoring him a ride this night, either. A carload of teenagers whizzed by, topping off the insult by laying on the horn as they passed him. It was at least twenty minutes before another vehicle came along. He stepped out and waved both arms this time, damn near getting himself killed. Whatever happened to *do unto others?* In places like this, decent people didn't leave each other stranded in the cold.

His face was feeling stiff, and he figured he'd better start walking before his toes went numb. He struck out for a distant yard light, the only sign of human habitation in sight. He couldn't tell how distant, but he knew he'd be hurting by the time he got there, and he was counting on some kindly old man to be answering the door. No shame among the lame.

It wasn't like Zach was fresh off the operating table—it had been a few months since his last round of repairs—but he hadn't given himself enough time. He'd lopped a couple of weeks off the near end of the doc's estimated recovery time, rigged up a brace, done some heavy-duty taping and climbed onto another bull. Hung in there for five seconds—four seconds past feeling the pop in his hip and three seconds short of the buzzer.

He could still feel the pain shooting down his leg with every step. Only this time he had to pick the damn thing up, swing it forward and drop it down again on his own.

Pride be damned, he just hoped *somebody* would be answering the door at the end of the road. The light in the front window was a good sign.

The four steps to the covered porch might as well have been four hundred, and he was looking to climb them with a lead weight chained to his left leg. His eyes were just as screwed up as his hip. Big black spots danced around with tiny red flashers, and he couldn't tell what was real and what wasn't. He stumbled over some shrubbery, steadied himself on the porch railing and peered between vertical slats.

There in the front window stood a spruce tree with a silver star affixed to the top. Zach was pretty sure the red sparks were all in his head, but the white lights twinkling by the hundreds throughout the huge tree, those were real. He wasn't too sure about the woman hanging the shiny balls. Most of her hair was caught up on her head and fastened in a surly clump, but the light captured by the escaped bits crowned her with a golden halo. Her face was a soft shadow, her body a willowy silhouette beneath a long white gown. If this was where the mind ran off to when cold started shutting down the rest of the body, then Zach's final worldly thought was, *This ain't such a bad way to go.*

If she would just turn to the window, he could die looking into the eyes of a Christmas angel.

* * * * *

Could this woman from Zach's past
get the lonesome cowboy to come in
from the cold…for good?
Look for
ONE COWBOY, ONE CHRISTMAS
by Kathleen Eagle
Available December 2009
from Silhouette Special Edition®.

Silhouette Desire

**FROM *NEW YORK TIMES*
BESTSELLING AUTHOR**

DIANA
PALMER

THE
MAVERICK

A BRAND-NEW
LONG, TALL
TEXAN STORY

SD76982

HARLEQUIN® HISTORICAL:
Where love is timeless

From chivalrous knights to roguish rakes, look for the variety Harlequin® Historical has to offer every month.

REQUEST YOUR FREE BOOKS!

2 FREE NOVELS PLUS 2 FREE GIFTS!

HARLEQUIN®

Blaze™

Red-hot reads!

YES! Please send me 2 FREE Harlequin® Blaze™ novels and my 2 FREE gifts (gifts are worth about $10). After receiving them, if I don't wish to receive any more books, I can return the shipping statement marked "cancel". If I don't cancel, I will receive 6 brand-new novels every month and be billed just $4.24 per book in the U.S. or $4.71 per book in Canada. That's a savings of 15% off the cover price. It's quite a bargain. Shipping and handling is just 50¢ per book.* I understand that accepting the 2 free books and gifts places me under no obligation to buy anything. I can always return a shipment and cancel at any time. Even if I never buy another book, the two free books and gifts are mine to keep forever.

151 HDN EYS2 351 HDN EYTE

Name _____ (PLEASE PRINT) _____

Address _____ Apt. # _____

City _____ State/Prov. _____ Zip/Postal Code _____

Signature (if under 18, a parent or guardian must sign)

Mail to the Harlequin Reader Service:
IN U.S.A.: P.O. Box 1867, Buffalo, NY 14240-1867
IN CANADA: P.O. Box 609, Fort Erie, Ontario L2A 5X3

Not valid to current subscribers of Harlequin Blaze books.

Want to try two free books from another line?
Call 1-800-873-8635 or visit www.morefreebooks.com.

* Terms and prices subject to change without notice. Prices do not include applicable taxes. N.Y. residents add applicable sales tax. Canadian residents will be charged applicable provincial taxes and GST. Offer not valid in Quebec. This offer is limited to one order per household. All orders subject to approval. Credit or debit balances in a customer's account(s) may be offset by any other outstanding balance owed by or to the customer. Please allow 4 to 6 weeks for delivery. Offer available while quantities last.

Your Privacy: Harlequin Books is committed to protecting your privacy. Our Privacy Policy is available online at www.eHarlequin.com or upon request from the Reader Service. From time to time we make our lists of customers available to reputable third parties who may have a product or service of interest to you. If you would prefer we not share your name and address, please check here. ☐

HB09R3

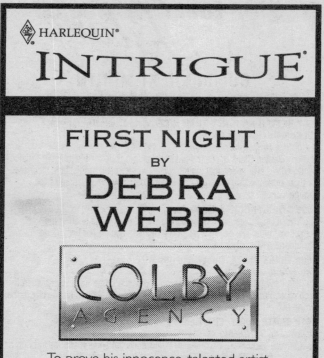

COMING NEXT MONTH

Available November 24, 2009

#507 BETTER NAUGHTY THAN NICE Vicki Lewis Thompson, Jill Shalvis, Rhonda Nelson
A Blazing Holiday Collection
Bad boy Damon Claus is determined to mess things up for his jolly big brother, Santa. Who'd ever guess that sibling rivalry would result in mistletoe madness for three unsuspecting couples! And Damon didn't even have to spike the eggnog....

#508 STARSTRUCK Julie Kenner
For Alyssa Chambers, having the perfect Christmas means snaring the perfect man. And she has him all picked out. Too bad it's her best friend, Christopher Hyde, who has her seeing stars.

#509 TEXAS BLAZE Debbi Rawlins
The Wrong Bed
Hot and heavy. That's how Kate Manning and Mitch Colter have always been for each other. But it's not till Kate makes the right move—though technically in the wrong bed—that things start heating up for good!

#510 SANTA, BABY Lisa Renee Jones
Dressed to Thrill, Bk. 4
As a blonde bombshell, Caron Avery thinks she's got enough attitude to bring a man to his knees. But when she seduces hot playboy Baxter Remington, will she be the one begging for more?

#511 CHRISTMAS MALE Cara Summers
Uniformly Hot!
All policewoman Fiona Gallagher wants for Christmas is a little excitement. But once she finds herself working on a case with sexy captain D. C. Campbell, she's suddenly aching for a different kind of thrill....

#512 TWELVE NIGHTS Hope Tarr
Blaze Historicals
Lady Alys is desperately in love with Scottish bad boy Callum Fraser. And keeping him out of her bed until the wedding is nearly killing her. So what's stopping them from indulging? Uhh...Elys's deceased first husband, a man very much alive.